FOR THE

It was over five years since Rachel and Joel had parted in anger and bitterness, and now they had met again and all the old hostile feelings were there still – if anything, they were more violent than ever. For Rachel was going to marry Joel's father, and Joel felt he could never forgive her. And he still didn't know her real reason for going through with this marriage . . .

Books you will enjoy
by ANNE MATHER

TAKE WHAT YOU WANT

Sophie was only a teenager, but she knew she would never love, had never loved, anyone but her stepbrother Robert. But her whole family, including Robert, disapproved, and hoped she would get over the feeling. Were they right – or was Sophie?

COME THE VINTAGE

Ryan's father had left her a half share of his prosperous vine-growing business, and the other half to a man she had never heard of, a Frenchman named Alain des Beaunes – on condition that they married each other. So, for the sake of the business, they married, neither caring anything for the other. Where did they go from there?

DARK VENETIAN

Emma ought to have known that her stepmother Celeste never did anything except for selfish reasons, and even a holiday in a Venetian *palazzo* could not compensate for the heartache she was to suffer. Celeste wanted to add a title to her wealth – but did it *have* to be Count Vidal Cesare, the man Emma herself loved?

DARK CASTLE

What Julie had once felt for Jonas Hunter was now past history and she had made every effort to keep it so. But now she found herself travelling to Scotland to make contact with him again. Could she manage to remain on purely business terms with the man who had meant so much to her and whose attraction for her had increased rather than lessened?

FOR THE LOVE OF SARA

BY

ANNE MATHER

MILLS & BOON LIMITED
17–19 FOLEY STREET
LONDON W1A 1DR

First published 1975
This edition 1975

ISBN 0 263 71900 6

Made and Printed in Great Britain by
C. Nicholls & Company Ltd.
The Philips Park Press, Manchester

CHAPTER ONE

JOEL left the motorway at the Salton turn-off and drove west into open country. Beyond the few villages which flanked the motorway, miles and miles of gorse-strewn moorland stretched before him, interspersed here and there with cottages, their smoking chimneys the only sign of habitation. There were sheep in plenty, of course, straying carelessly on to the road in front of him so that he was continually bearing down on the brake, and the impatience that filled him at the necessity for this journey grew with every second wasted. At any other time, the artistic sensitivity which had ensured his success in his chosen profession would have responded to the almost miraculous blending of colour as evening had shadowed the slanting rays of the sun. The pale turquoise of the horizon now the sun had set shimmered with the approaching dusk and set the stars trembling. But right now Joel's thoughts were much less pleasantly occupied, and he felt no affinity with this wind-swept landscape, only irritation that his destination was so remote from the civilisation he was used to. The occasional cars that passed him going in the opposite direction were forced to remove themselves from their positions on the crown of the road by the sheer width of the Mercedes, and he reflected broodingly that drivers around here apparently considered they had the free and only rights to the highway. He was not in a mood to be generous in this direction; his stomach was telling him he hadn't eaten since breakfast, and he longed for a drink to cool his frustration.

He glanced at the plain gold watch on his wrist. It was already past seven o'clock. It would be night soon, and he had no desire to negotiate these roads after dark. It was incredible to think that only a little over an hour ago he had been bypassing the industrial centres of Doncaster and Leeds when now he seemed distant from everything urban. That was why he hadn't stopped earlier although the service areas on the motorway had mocked his good sense. He estimated he had only another five or six miles to go to Langthwaite, and with a bit of luck the hotel there would be able to supply all his needs. At least, until tomorrow.

He sighed and flexed the fingers of first one hand, then the other. It had been after two when he left London, so he supposed he had made reasonable time. He hadn't rushed, but again he hadn't wasted time. He had been singularly reluctant to reach his destination when he set off, and although that had changed, his feelings were definitely mixed. Deep inside him there was a hard core of bitterness about the whole affair, and no amount of soul-searching would convince him he was doing the right thing. He had said he would do it for Francis' sake, but was that entirely true

He shifted irritably, unwilling to investigate his motives. He was here now, he had to go through with it. Twilight was deepening, but there were lights up ahead and he turned on the car's lights to read the sign. He almost missed it, a gravestone-like fixture at the side of the road, half hidden by the long grass. He wondered if the connotation was significant and then shook his head impatiently. This was no time for self-doubt or self-delusion.

The village was small, a collection of cottages clustered about a cobbled square. There was the inevitable telephone box outside the post office, a general dealers, which looked as though it sold everything, but probably didn't, and the inn. The Golden Pheasant! Joel's mouth turned down at the corners. It made a change from the Black Bull or the Bay Horse, he supposed. It certainly did not have the appearance of a five-star hostelry, but if the beds were clean and the beer was cold, he would have no objections.

There were one or two teenagers loafing about in the square, and the sight of the sleek cream Mercedes attracted a few coarse comments. Joel was forced to leave the car outside the inn, trusting to God and providence that no one would run a rusty nail along its side. Where was the age-old rustic charm he had imagined? Gone like everything else beneath the heel of indifference? At least there was no regimented housing estate encroaching on the village boundaries, and it was too far from the nearest town to attract evening commuters.

Leaving his one case in the boot, Joel pulled his sheepskin jacket on over his shirt and pants, and sliding the knot of his tie up to his collar he entered the bar entrance which appeared to be the only means of access. It was still comparatively early in the evening, and there were only one or two elderly patrons occupying the tables in the bar, but the girl who was serving was young, and pretty too if you liked buxom blondes. She was obviously intrigued by the appearance of a dark stranger, and Joel could feel her assessing him from the thickness of his straight hair to the soles of his suede boots. What she saw she apparently approved of, because the look she bestowed on him was warm and encouraging.

"Yes, sir? What will it be?"

Joel hesitated, then he drew his wallet out of his inside pocket. "Oh – er – I'll have a beer." He glanced round. "You do take overnight visitors here, don't you?"

The girl filled his glass and pushed the foaming beverage across to him. Her eyes had widened and she was regarding him curiously now. "Overnight visitors, sir? At the inn? Well, I think Mr. Harris takes one or two. I'm not sure whether at this time of year . . ." She handed him the change from a pound note, holding his gaze with her own. "Would you like me to find out for you?"

Joel slid the silver into his pocket. "If you wouldn't mind," he agreed, raising the glass to his lips and drinking thirstily.

The girl regarded him for another inquisitive moment, and then with a shrug she turned and went out. Joel lowered his weight on to a bar stool. The beer was good – cold, as he liked it, and refreshing after his hours at the wheel. He was aware that his presence was causing a minor argument in the corner between two of the older patrons, and he guessed they got few visitors in Langthwaite at this time of year.

The girl was coming back and with her was a middle-aged man, obviously the licensee. Joel forced a smile and had it doubtfully returned. "You're wanting accommodation, I hear," Mr. Harris stated, leaning on the bar. "Would it be for long?"

"One night only, I expect," replied Joel evenly.

"You're a traveller, then, sir?" suggested the older man, curiously, but Joel shook his head.

"I – I have business in Langthwaite," he conceded, realising that by saying nothing he was likely to be turned away. "Can you put me up?"

"Well, it's nothing fancy like," retorted Mr. Harris. "There is a room you can have. My wife's making up the bed now. Would you be wanting meals as well?"

Joel restrained the impulse to swear. Of course he wanted meals. Did they think he was without the normal demands of the human body? "If – that's possible," he remarked, with admirable calmness. "Naturally, I don't expect your wife to put herself out for one guest. Some sandwiches this evening would do fine, and perhaps some toast in the morning."

Mrs. Harris, or at least Joel assumed it was that lady, appeared behind them. "Is this the gentleman who is wanting to stay the night?" she asked, and her husband nodded. "Very well, sir. Your room's ready. And I expect you're hungry, aren't you?"

"I – well –" Joel looked helplessly at Mr. Harris, and

he nodded with a finality that displayed a decision made.

"Yes, Ellie. The gentleman – I don't know your name, do I, sir? – he is hungry–"

"Kingdom," said Joel at once, "Joel Kingdom. From London."

In what seemed a remarkably short space of time, he was shown to his room on the first floor, given free use of the bathroom, and then fed in a tiny dining room which he suspected was generally only used by the family. Mrs. Harris herself served him, although the blonde from the bar found the excuse to pop in and out asking him whether he had everything he wanted. Joel, who was used to the effect his swarthy attraction had on the opposite sex, found her obvious charms less than appealing, and his mouth was wry by the time he had eaten soup, cold roast beef and pickles, and a piece of Mrs. Harris's crusty apple pie.

Mrs. Harris herself bustled in as he was finishing the lager he had had with the meal and she looked gratified at his empty plate. "You enjoyed it, then, sir?"

Joel nodded, massaging the aching muscles of his left shoulder. "It was very good, thank you, Mrs. Harris. You've been very kind."

Mrs. Harris beamed, her plump face mirroring her pleasure. "And you're only staying until tomorrow?" she asked, beginning to gather the dirty dishes together.

Joel rose to his feet. "I hope so." Then, as she quickly looked up, he added: "I mean, of course, I hope my business doesn't take longer than that." He sighed. "I have to get back to London."

"You work in London, Mr. Kingdom?"

"Sometimes." Joel was non-committal.

"But your home's there?"

"You could say that."

Mrs. Harris was clearly trying to find an opening to ask

what business he had in Langthwaite, and Joel was equally unwilling to assist her. He suppressed a yawn with his hand, and said:

"If you don't mind, Mrs. Harris, I'll go up to my room now. It's been a long day, and I am rather tired."

Mrs. Harris hid her frustration. "Of course, sir. You know where it is?"

"Of course." Joel smiled, and the woman responded to the spreading charm it generated. "I'll say goodnight, then."

"Goodnight, sir." Mrs. Harris smiled in return, and Joel turned to cross the hall to the stiarcase.

The blonde appeared in the doorway to the bar. "Aren't you coming back for another drink?" she asked him coyly.

Joel shook his head. "No, thank you."

"You're never going to bed!"

"Why not? It is after ten o'clock, you know."

"Mercy me! Ten o'clock!" The girl raised her eyes heavenward. "I thought you Londoners were used to late hours. What's happened to the swinging seventies?"

"I think they hanged themselves," returned Joel dryly. "Goodnight."

His room was under the eaves, and the ceiling sloped towards the window. He could stand upright just inside the door, but from then on it was a losing battle. Still, the bed looked long and comfortable, and he would be glad to stretch his aching limbs. That work-out in the gym that morning had been intended to relax his mind as well as his body, but the way he felt right now it hadn't succeeded in either direction.

The bathroom didn't sport a shower, but he ran a shallow bath and sluiced himself before going back to his bedroom. Then he removed his robe, turned out the light and slid between the cotton sheets. The bed was icily cold. The inn was not centrally heated. But the heat generated by his thoughts soon warmed him through.

He lay on his back with his arms behind his head and stared grimly towards the shadowy flowers visible on the cretonne of the curtains. So – he was here, in Langthwaite, and somewhere out there, within a mile's radius, was Rachel – Rachel *Gilmour* as she called herself now, but Rachel just the same.

Bitterness brought the sickly taste of bile to the back of his throat. That Rachel should think she could do *this*, to *him!* His hands balled themselves into fists. If he had her here now, he thought, he would wring her neck!

But such passion was wasted, and he knew it. Coolness and calmness, and a sense of objectivity would serve him far better. After all, he could not be absolutely sure she was doing it to spite him, although the alternative was equally unpalatable . . .

He deliberately unclenched his fists and forced the muscles of his neck to relax. Was it really only three days ago that Francis had come to him with the story? It seemed as though he had known it for much longer than that.

He had been working, he remembered, putting the finishing touches to the portrait of Lady Antonia Barrie, when Francis came hammering at his door. He had not been pleased at the intrusion. He had got up especially early to take advantage of the light, and when his half-brother interrupted him he had been less than civil. It wasn't until Francis had stammered out the story in that way he had when he was distressed that Joel realised this wasn't another of the simple monetary scrapes Francis had often got himself into.

Even then he had been loath to get involved. "But I don't see why you should imagine the fact that our father is thinking of getting married again should trouble me!" he had declared impatiently.

Francis, as tall as himself but thinner, fairer, had paced restlessly about Joel's studio. "Of course, it wouldn't bother you, would it?" he had demanded fiercely. "Your grandmother left you more than adequately provided for. Unfortunately,

I don't have rich relations like that on my mother's side. And if Father marries again, why shouldn't he disinherit me, as he disinherited you?"

Joel had raked his hair back from his forehead with frustrated hands. "That didn't trouble you too much at the time," he observed dryly. Then: "It was different with me, Fran, you know it was! Father could never see that I wasn't cut out to play power politics at the Bank. And, as you say, my grandmother made Father's participation in my career less than necessary. You're different, Fran. You're his son. And even if he does marry again, which I personally doubt, there's little chance now that he'll sire more children. Good God, he's sixty-three!"

Francis turned on him then. "Men have been known to have children at ninety, and you know it!" He paused, his face changing, becoming more calculating. "Besides," he regarded his half brother scornfully, "you haven't heard it all yet. You haven't asked who the woman might be."

Joel shrugged. "Does it matter?"

"It might. Her name is Gilmour, Rachel Gilmour." He hesitated, enjoying the effect his words were having. "Her name was Rachel Abbey before she married her first husband!"

And that was when Joel had crossed the studio and done something entirely uncharacteristic. He had caught his haf-brother by his shirt front and dragging him up close to him said savagely: "What are you saying?"

Francis, abashed by his older brother's intimidation, had struggled to free himself. "It – it – it's the – t-truth, Jo-Joel! It – it is – Ra-Rachel, it – it is!"

Joel had released him so violently that Francis had spun across the studio and landed on the floor amidst a pile of canvases and an easel. His face had twisted angrily as he got to his feet, and as he brushed his clothes he had stared maliciously at his brother.

"It – it's not m-my fault!" he muttered, grimacing as his stammer continued. "Just – just because – you d–don't like the – tr–truth when you – hear it!"

Joel had hardly been listening to him. He believed Francis all right. He wouldn't come here with a story like that unless he had proof that it was true. But that didn't make it any better. Searching for a cheroot amongst a mess of paints and sketches on the long board beneath the window, he put one between his teeth and lit it with hands that were no longer steady. Then he stared grimly out of the window for several silent minutes, looking over the rooftops of London to the curve of the Thames in the distance. When he had himself under some semblance of control he turned back to Francis. The younger man had lit a cigarette and was puffing at it nervously, but his expression was defiant when Joel said:

"Tell me what you know," in low uncompromising tones.

Francis shifted from one foot to the other. "I'm not sure I want to tell you anything," he muttered.

Joel's jaw stiffened. "Don't tempt me, Francis," he said, in the same low tone. "Now, how do you know it's – Rachel?"

"I've seen her!"

"You've – *what*!"

"I – I've seen her. Oh, for God's sake, Joel, stop looking at me like that! It's not my – f–fault."

"Go on. Where did you see her?"

"L–last night. With – with Father! It – it's true!" This as Joel threw his cheroot to the floor and ground it under his heel. "They – they were – d–dining together."

"Where?" Joel took a step towards him, and Francis took a step backward.

"At – at – Peruccios. I – I saw them, I tell you."

Joel moved his head disbelievingly from side to side.

"Start at the beginning."

Francis drew heavily on his cigarette, and blew the smoke into the air above their heads. "Well – well, I've – I've known for some time that – that there was a woman . . . oh, yes, I have. Since – since my mother left – I've always been able to tell."

"For the Lord's sake, get to the point!"

"Well – well, about – about a week ago, Father told me that – that there was someone –"

"But you didn't choose to tell me that!"

"Not immediately, no!" Francis was defensive. "Joel, as you've just pointed out, he's sixty-three! I assumed – who wouldn't have? – that – that this women, whoever she might be, would be a contemporary of his! After all, you have to admit, both your mother and mine were near his own age at the time he married them."

"All right, all right. Go on."

"Well, I didn't say much, I didn't ask much. He told me – oh, how he must have laughed when he told me – that her name was Mrs. Gilmour, Mrs. Rachel Gilmour. Rachel's not such an uncommon name, is it?"

"And that was all?"

"No. No, he said – she came from Yorkshire. That – that she worked in a village called – Langth – whistle, Langthwaite – something like that – as – as a housekeeper to a retired colonel."

"A housekeeper to a retired colonel!" Joel repeated the words sceptically.

"Yes. Yes, that's what he said!"

"You must have made a mistake –"

"I tell you, I saw her –"

"Not about that. About – what she's doing." Joel's fists clenched. "Francis, you know Rachel was at college – when – when –"

"When she walked out on you? I know. But how do you

know she finished her training? That – that was six years ago. She – she's been married. She – she's got a child!"

"*A child*?" Joel's tanned face was pale. "Did Father tell you this too?"

"Y – yes." Francis stubbed out his cigarette in an onyx ashtray. Then he looked up. "Th–that might account for the fact that she's someone's housekeeper, mightn't it? I mean, it's not easy to get jobs with – with children."

"And – her husband?" Joel's eyes were narrowed beneath heavy lids.

Francis shrugged. "How should I know? Dead, I suppose. Father said she was a – a widow!"

"*A widow*?" Joel paced restlessly across the room. "I don't believe it!" He swung round on his half-brother. "Are you sure this isn't all some malicious trick to get his own way?"

"Wh–what do you mean?"

Joel shook his head. "I don't know, I don't know. Father always hated me for thwarting him –"

"I don't think he hates you, Joel –"

"Don't you? I do. I think he'd marry Rachel just for that reason."

"You're crazy!"

"Am I?" Joel's expression was broodingly malevolent. "If I thought..." He broke off. "Is that all?"

"What – what more can I tell you?"

"What did Father say when he told you?"

"I've told you everything I know."

"Except how you came to see them together last night."

Francis sighed. "That was accidental. Father doesn't know I saw them."

"So?"

"I was going to Freddi's," he named a gambling establishment with which Joel was not unfamiliar, "but I was short on funds –"

"– as usual –"

"– and I suddenly remembered Perry Simons." Perry Simons owned Peruccios. Joel knew this, too. "I went round there. I was going to ask him for a loan. Then I saw them."

"And you left?"

"Yes."

"What time was that?"

Francis glanced at his watch. "Around eleven."

"And it's eight-thirty now. What have you been doing for nine and a half hours?"

Francis shook his head. "I – I didn't know wh-what to do. I – I didn't kn-know wh-whether to t-tell you or not."

"Why not?"

Francis shook his head. "I w-walked for m-miles. I ended up b-back at the fl-flat at about four. I would have r-rung you then, but I th-thought you m-might be – other – otherwise engaged."

His meaning was not lost on Joel, and his lips twisted. He gave a final look at Lady Antonia's portrait and then walked across the studio to the door leading into the main body of the penthouse. "Okay," he said heavily. "I'll make some coffee. I gave Heron the night off, so he won't be in until later. We can talk just as well in the kitchen."

Later that day, Joel had learned that Rachel, if it was Rachel as Francis insisted, had returned to Yorkshire. He found his father was not averse to talking about Mrs. Gilmour when he discovered that his younger son had told Joel of his plans. Joel was forced to bite his tongue and control his fists when confronting his father's smug countenance, and indeed, if he had had any lingering doubts as to the veracity of Francis's story, they were dispersed by that interview with his father. James Kingdom was obviously well pleased with himself, and Joel found his anger turning against Rachel with destructive violence. How could she? he had asked himself again and again. How could she think of doing this to him? And the answer came back that she hated him now as he was beginning to hate her.

Nevertheless, he could not let it happen, just like that. He found himself championing Francis's rights, and refusing to admit his motives were less than unselfish. If Rachel had already been married and had produced a child, she had proved she was fertile, and his father was still a powerful and virile man. Two wives were enough for any man, thought Joel bitterly, without acknowledging that had his own mother not died soon after his birth, his father might only have had one.

But that was three days ago now. In that time, Francis had managed to find out that Rachel's employer was a Colonel Frenshaw, who lived at the Old Hall, Langthwaite. A not-too-difficult place to find, Joel had thought, until he began this journey...

He turned restlessly in the narrow bed, wishing himself back in his own bed in his own apartment. He had told no one but Francis and his man, Heron, of his real motives for coming to Yorkshire, and he had no doubts that Erica would be curious on his return. Erica...

He determinedly brought the image of the girl he would no doubt marry one day to his mind. Six years had drawn a distorting veil over Rachel's features, and although he could remember the details of her appearance it was hard to put them in the right perspective. Besides, he didn't particularly want to remember Rachel, until he had to...

Six years. It was a long time. She would be what? Twenty-four or twenty-five by now. He should remember. She was ten years younger than he was. He sighed, recalling how amazed he had been that a girl of her age should have had the power over him that she had had. Power that she had abused, he told himself savagely. Well, all that was in the past. No woman, either before or since, had had that kind of power-that kind of control over him, nor ever would again. When he met her tomorrow, or perhaps *confronted* was a better word, she would soon realise she had bitten off more than she could chew by challenging him like this. How could she? he asked himself again; how *dared* she imagine she could make herself a member of his family without arousing any reaction from him? Or perhaps that was exactly what she wanted to achieve. The idea struck him forcibly, leaving him cold with anger. And no doubt his father was a willing accomplice.

Yet still he couldn't believe it. But what other conclusion could he draw? He turned his head restlessly into the pillow and wished he had had that last drink in the bar. A strong double whisky might have soothed his nerves, dulled the sharp edge of exhaustion that was keeping him awake, cast into oblivion the destructive desire for revenge which was tearing him apart.

CHAPTER TWO

At breakfast the next morning it was a simple matter to ask Mrs. Harris where the Old Hall was situated.

"Colonel Frenshaw's place?" she asked, raising her eyebrows. "You're a friend of his, Mr. Kingdom?"

Joel attacked his grapefruit with more determination than enthusiasm. "Not exactly, Mrs. Harris. I – er – I do know someone who works for him, though."

"Oh, that would be Mr. Hanson, would it, sir?"

Joel's head jerked up. Pushing the straight hair off his forehead, he frowned. "Hanson? No, I know no one of that name, Mrs. Harris."

Mrs. Harris pursed her lips. "Oh, don't you?" she shrugged. "I thought as how you might. Mr. Hanson, he's the Colonel's secretary, see. Educated young chap, he is. Gets in here sometimes of a weekend."

Joel's frown deepened. "Indeed?" He hesitated. "No. The person – the person I know is, I believe, Colonel Frenshaw's housekeeper."

Mrs. Harris's face cleared, but she was surprised, and looked it. "Young Mrs. Gilmour?" she exclaimed.

Joel looked down at the grapefruit again. "That's right."

Mrs. Harris raised her eyebrows. "I don't know the young lady, except to say hello to. She doesn't come in here, and being the publican's wife, I don't get out a lot."

"No, of course not." Joel's brain was working furiously. "Are – are there other – members of staff? At the Hall, I mean?"

"Not as I know of, sir. There's just the Colonel, and Mr.,

Hanson, and Mrs. Gilmour, of course. Oh, and the little girl Sara."

Joel felt his nerves prickle. "Mrs. – Gilmour's – child?"

"Yes. But of course, you'd know that."

Joel made no reply. So the child was a girl, Sara. He shook his head. He couldn't imagine Rachel being old enough to be a mother. And yet . . .

"You were going to tell me where the Old Hall is situated," he reminded Mrs. Harris.

She nodded, taking away the half eaten dish of grapefruit and replacing it with a plate of ham, eggs, sausages and tomatoes. Ordinarily Joel would have done full justice to such a meal, but this morning after his restless night, the fried breakfast looked nauseating. Nevertheless, he had to make an effort, and tackled the bacon first.

"If you follow the Cragstone road for about a mile, you'll come across it, sir. On your left. You can't miss it. It's the only house for miles."

"Thank you."

Joel poured himself some coffee and drank slowly. It was half past eight. Was nine o'clock too early to go calling? He had contemplated telephoning first, but dismissed the idea. He wanted to see Rachel's face when she saw him. He wanted to feel the surge of satisfaction that would come when he confronted her with his contempt.

He ate sparingly, much to Mrs. Harris's disappointment, but he thanked her warmly for the meal and her hospitality, and added a not ungenerous gratuity to the bill. Then he collected his belongings from his room and carried them out to the car.

It was an unexpectedly mild morning for early March, and he decided to stow his sheepskin coat in the boot and wear instead the jacket that matched his dark blue suede pants. Sliding his arms into the sleeves of his jacket, he surveyed the village square with more enthusiasm. Seen in the light of a strengthening sun, it had a certain charm which he had missed the night before. He noticed that there were daffodils and narcissi growing in every available patch of earth, and all the buildings had a scrubbed, well-cared-for appearance. A couple of dogs were scratching beside the drinking fountain that formed part of the wall that edged the churchyard, and even as he stood there the church clock chimed the hour. He glanced quickly at his watch. The time had come, and he wished he felt more prepared for it.

Unlocking the door, he slid behind the wheel of the Mercedes sports. The engine fired at the first flick of his wrist, and a faint smile of satisfaction momentarily dispelled the deep lines beween his brows.

With Mrs. Harris's directions, it was not difficult to find the Cragstone road, and not far outside the village he came upon a rambling stone building which could only be the Old Hall. Smoke drifted from chimneys so obviously someone was up and about, and an old station wagon was parked on the forecourt. Rusty wrought iron gates hung half off their hinges leaving the entrance wide for anyone to drive through. Joel had stopped just outside the gates, undecided whether to leave the car there or not, but then, with a characteristic shrug of his shoulders, he released the brake and drove between the gateposts, and cruised along the gravel drive to stop beside the station wagon.

His arrival aroused no immediate response beyond a half-hearted barking from the back of the house. He got out of the car and stood for a moment looking up at the blank windows. So this was where Rachel had lived – how long? The last two – three years, maybe? He flexed his shoulder muscles. Since her husband died, no doubt. Francis had said she was a widow. And Gilmour? Who was Gilmour? What had this man been who had married her so briefly? Why had she married him? Because she loved him? If so, love came more easily to her than it had done to him . . .

He flung the thoughts aside, and walked round the two vehicles to the porch. A bellrope invited usage, and with a tautening of his stomach muscles, he pulled, hard. The sound echoed and re-echoed throughout the house and he hoped that no one was sleeping in there. The noise would awaken the dead.

He waited. For a few minutes he began to think that either no one was in or no one was up. But the smoking chimneys and the station wagon seemed to negate such an idea. And indeed, after an interminable time footsteps sounded across the hall beyond the half fluted glass door and presently it was opened. A young man stood regarding him expectantly, a thin, reddish-haired young man, with a small beard and moustache that were no doubt intended to give his face maturity. "Yes?"

Joel was taken aback. He had half expected Rachel to open the door, and now she hadn't he was temporarily speechless. Then he gathered himself, and said shortly: "I'd like to speak to Mrs. Gilmour."

"Rachel?"

The young man raised his eyebrows, and there was a touch of hostility in the way he said her name. Joel felt a ridiculous temptation to grab him by his collar and demand whether he had been given the right to use her Christian name, but instead he replied: "Yes, that's right. Rachel."

The young man was definitely hostile now. "I'm afraid she's busy at the moment," he said. "Perhaps you could call back later."

Joel contained his impatience. "Just tell her that there's a Mr. Kingdom asking to speak to her," he said. "I think you'll find she'll speak to me."

"Kingdom?" The young man regarded him coldly. "You're some relation of – James Kingdom, then?"

"Not that it's any business of yours, but yes." Joel put one foot on the threshold. "Now, will you please deliver my message?"

The young man shrugged and turned away to cross the parquet flooring of the wide entrance hall. Joel rested his shoulder against the doorpost and watched him sourly. That, of course, was the Hanson fellow Mrs. Harris had spoken about. He was younger than he had expected. He wondered what his relationship was with Rachel.

He half turned and looked back across the gardens edging the drive. Someone had taken the trouble to mow the lawn quite recently, and the rhododendrons would be quite beautiful when they were out. Something was jutting from beneath the rhododendron bushes, something that had once been red, but which was now streaked with dirt and dried leaves. It looked like a wheelbarrow, a very small wheelbarrow. A toy wheelbarrow, in fact. His lips twisted. The child – Sara's – no doubt.

"You wanted to see me?"

The low voice sounded right behind him, and his head jerked round almost of its own volition. He had not heard her approach, but Rachel was standing just inside the doorway, her hands thrust into the pockets of the gingham apron she was wearing over shabby slacks and an open-necked shirt blouse. Her face was thinner than he remembered, unnaturally flushed in places and pale as death in others; her body was thinner, too, but her hair, the silky ash-blonde glory of her hair which he had always found such a sensual pleasure in burying his face in, was still as beautiful as ever, albeit unattractively confined at the moment in a severe knot at the nape of her neck. Joel straightened slowly, allowing his eyes to move over her in a deliberately insolent way, and was faintly gratified by the way she shifted under his gaze.

"Well, well," he remarked mockingly. "Mrs. Gilmour, as I live and breathe."

"What do you want, Joel? I'm employed here, and I have work to do."

She spoke quickly, breathily, and she cast a fleeting glance over her shoulder as she did so. That was when Joel saw the man, Hanson, lurking in the background, and his patience snapped.

"Get rid of the watchdog and come outside and talk to me!" he snapped harshly. "We have things to say to one another which I don't intend to discuss under Mrs. Grundy's gaze!"

"Rachel –"

Hanson would have come forward then, but she gestured for him to keep out of this. "Joel, I realise you think you require an explanation –"

"You're damn right, I do!"

"Your father promised he wouldn't tell you –"

"Oh, did he? Big of him!"

"– and now he has –"

"Correction – Francis saw you together."

"Oh, *God*!"

"He won't help you now!" Joel glared coldly at her. "Now, do you get rid of your boy-friend, or do I?"

"Joel, I mean it!" she exclaimed unsteadily. "I – I can't talk to you now. Colonel Frenshaw is waiting for his breakfsat, and – and –"

"Rachel, I warn you –"

She wrung her hands then. "All right, Joel, all right. I will talk to you. But not now. Not here. Not like this." She glanced behind her again. "C–could you come back later? This – this afternoon, perhaps?"

Joel thrust his hands into his jacket pockets. If he hadn't he felt sure he would have taken hold of her and shaken her until her teeth chattered. Standing there, talking about getting Colonel Frenshaw's breakfast, when he had driven over two hundred miles to get the truth out of her. But losing his temper, making a scene here, would do no good. In fact she would be quite within her rights to refuse to speak to him again, and he had no rights here whatsoever. This was private property. Without anyone's permission to remain, he was trespassing, and Hanson would see to it that Rachel was made aware of this.

Controlling himself with difficulty, he said: "Very well, this afternoon. What time?"

Rachel gave a nervous shrug. "I don't know. Two o'clock – half past?"

"Two o'clock," agreed Joel grimly, and without trusting himself to say another word, he strode back to his car. The door had closed before he had started the engine and he pressed his foot hard down on the accelerator and had the childish pleasure of spraying the station wagon with the gravel torn up by his rear wheels.

He spent the morning by a beck he found a few miles further along the road to Cragstone. He didn't return to Langthwaite even when the natural demands of his body required relief, and although he was hungry by one o'clock he contented himself with a cheroot and a can of beer he kept in the glove compartment for emergencies. The beer was warm, and he grimaced as he wiped his mouth with the back of his hand. If there was one thing he detested it was warm beer.

But it was pleasant by the beck, and the sun was warm on his face as he stretched his length on the bracken. If Erica had been with him she would no doubt have been chiding him for risking ruining his clothes in this way, but then Erica, being in the fashion business, was always conscious of appearances.

At a quarter to two he got up, brushed himself down, and walked back ot the car. The sky had become overcast within the last half hour, and even as he stepped into the vehicle he felt a spot of rain touch his face. Grimacing at the weather, he reversed out on to the road and turned back towards Langthwaite. By the time he reached the rise from which he could see the sprawling grey mass of the Hall below him, it was raining quite heavily, and he hoped Rachel would not expect the weather to deter him.

He drew up beside the shabby station wagon just after two o'clock, and instead of getting out of the car to go to the door, he sounded the horn. It was an arrogant thing to do, and he knew it, but his feelings would not allow him any weakness or compassion.

Minutes passed, and no one came, and his temper simmered. Damn the woman, where was she? She knew he would come. Why the hell hadn't she been waiting for him? But he knew deep inside him that Rachel was not likely to be intimidated by what she would term an immature attempt to disconcert her.

With a sigh, he thrust open his door and got out, scowling as within seconds his shoulders were wet. He ran for the porch, and as he reached it, the door opened and Rachel appeared. She looked surprised to see him, but he was convinced she had been waiting for him to get out of the car before showing herself.

He sheltered in the porchway as she closed the door behind her, his expression not encouraging. "Very clever!" he observed coldly. "But rather childish, don't you think?"

She looked up at him with wide, innocent hazel eyes. "What are you talking about?"

Joel opened his mouth to berate her, and then closed it again. He shook his head, and glanced briefly at her clothes. She was still wearing the shirt and slacks from the morning, but the apron had been replaced by a fur-lined poplin coat. Its dark green colour accentuated the pallor of her cheeks, and for a moment compassion stirred within him.

"Do you want me to bring the car nearer?" he asked.

She shook her head now. "I'm used to walking in the rain," she replied. "Shall we go?"

Taking the initiative, she stepped out from the porch, and with a suppressed oath, Joel strode ahead of her to open the car doors. She got into the front seat without looking at him, and he slammed the door more violently than was necessary before walking round the bonnet to join her.

Once inside, he examined the shoulders of his jacket, and finding them soaked, he took his jacket off and slung it carelessly on to the back seat. Then he indicated that she might like to do the same, but she silently refused. Shrugging, he started the engine and drove down the drive, halting at the gates when she said:

"Where are you taking me? I have to be back in an hour."

"An hour?" He glared sideways at her.

"Yes, an hour. Sara sleeps for that long in the afternoons. I have to be back before she awakes."

Joel made no comment, but drove swiftly along the road towards the spot where he had parked this morning. There was room there to park the car off the road, and it was remote enough, goodness knows. Rachel said nothing as they drove along, and Joel wondered whether she was composing what she was going to say to him. For himself, anger simmered too near the surface for him to think with reasonable logic, and he had to force himself not to stop the car there and then and demand that she stop this ridiculous charade she was playing.

It didn't take long to reach the beck, and Joel stopped the car on the layby and reached automatically for a cheroot. Without asking her permission, he lit it and inhaled deeply, rolling down his window half way to allow the fumes to escape.

"Well?" he said at last, when she still made no attempt to speak to him. "What's it all about?"

Rachel linked her hands together in her lap. "What's what all about?"

"Don't give me that, Rachel. We both know what I'm talking about. I want to know how you came to know my father well enough for him to ask you to marry him."

Rachel lifted her slim shoulders. "I – I've known him for years, Joel. You know that."

Joel chewed impatiently at the end of the cheroot. "Because I introduced you?" He scowled. "That won't do, Rachel. I can count on one hand the number of times you met my father through me. We were not – we have never been – the best of friends, and you know it!"

"I – I was only explaining that – that it's some years since I first met him, that's all."

"I am aware of that."

"I know you are." She curled her nails into her palms. "W-Why should it strike you as so extraordinary that your father should want to – to marry me? He – he always – liked me."

Joel's mouth thinned. "Rachel, for God's sake –"

"Oh, Joel, stop it! *Stop it!*" She put her hands over her ears. "Why did you come here? What do you hope to achieve? Everything between us was over long ago. You know that. You have no right to question what I intend to do."

"Haven't I?" Joel stared at her furiously. "Haven't I, just! My God, you're a cool one! Did you really think you could agree to marry *my* father without arousing any reaction from me?"

"What's it to do with you?"

"You want to be my stepmother, is that it? You love my father now as you once said you loved me? Oh, come off it, Rachel, it won't do! What is it? Some rotten attempt at revenge? Is this intended to show me what might have been?"

"And what if it is?" she burst out hotly. "What can you do about it?"

There was silence for a few moments and Joel stared grimly out of the windows at the falling rain. He couldn't believe it! He simply couldn't believe it! Rachel wasn't like that. Or at least, she hadn't been. But then it was years since they had split up. She had married since then, had a child. Who knew what manner of life she had led to bring her to this.

With a sigh he said quietly: "Tell me why you disappeared like that. What did I do to arouse such a desire to escape?"

Rachel took a deep breath. "You ask me that?" She shook her head bitterly. "What's the use of talking, Joel? The past is dead. It's the future I'm concerned about."

Joel's jaw hardened. "At anyone's expense!"

"That's not true. You know nothing about it."

"Then tell me."

Rachel pleated the folds of her coat. "Joel, I'm going to marry your father. Nothing you – or Francis – can say will alter that."

Joel's fists clenched. "You must be pretty desperate, Rachel!" he muttered savagely.

"I am."

"Why?" He turned to look at her, noticing again the hollows in her cheeks, the lacklustre quality of her eyes. Hardly the face of a bride-to-be. "Is it money? If it's money you want, I can give you that."

Rachel's lips twisted contemptuously. "If I were a man, I'd knock you down for a remark like that!" she exclaimed. "I wouldn't marry any man for money! Oh, you should be proud of yourself, Joel! You're a bastard of the first water!"

Joel moved then, imprisoning her wrist between his fingers, feeling the fragile bones quiver within his hand. He knew he could crush her physically with very little effort, but that was not his intention. He was not an animal. He had a brain, and he intended to use it. But just as this moment he wanted to hurt her, he wanted to see her squirm, as mentally she was trying to make him. She winced as he applied pressure to her wrist, but she didn't cry out. He was so close he could inhale the warm scent of her body, and his eyes were irresistibly drawn to the opened neck of her blouse. He understood only too well the fire that suddenly stirred in his loins, and with a feeling of self-disgust he let her go and slumped in his seat.

"I want to know about your husband and the child," he persisted doggedly. "Is Gilmour dead? My father said you're a widow."

Rachel was rubbing her wrist. "I am."

"What was your husband's name?"

"His name?" She looked startled. "You know his name."

"Gilmour?" Joel turned cold eyes on her. "Is that what you called him? Gilmour?"

"Oh! Oh, no, of course not." Rachel flushed then. "His Christian name was – Alan."

"Alan Gilmour. What did he do?" Rachel looked puzzled, and he added: "His occupation? What was his occupation?"

"Does it matter?"

"I think so."

She sighed. "He was an engineer. He – he worked for the government."

"I see." Joel digested this. "How long were you married?"

"Two – three years. What does it matter now?"

Joel didn't altogether understand why he was so curious, except that there was a certain sadistic satisfaction to be gained from forcing her to talk about something which must be painful to her. He threw the end of his cheroot out of the window. "I suppose you must have found it hard bringing up a child alone," he remarked probingly. "Is that why you took the job as this Colonel Frenshaw's housekeeper?" He paused. "Is that why you're marrying my father? For Sara's sake?"

"Don't you dare to mention her name!" she cried fiercely. "You don't know her. You don't know me. Why don't you go away and leave me alone!"

"I want to know."

"It's not your affair."

"Damn you, isn't it? I have a right to know – "

"A right! A right, Joel!" Her voice had risen. "You have no rights, no rights at all. You forfeited them when . . . when . . ." Her voice trailed away and she turned away from him, staring down at her hands. "I want to go back now. Will you take me – *please*?"

Joel levered himself up in his seat, staring at her averted profile. For a moment, just for a moment, he had been near to learning the real truth behind all this. He *knew* it, and he exulted in it. But she had withdrawn again, and frustration filled him. He sat there, his fists clenched, wishing for once that she was a man. With a man, he would have felt no compunction about beating the truth out of him. But Rachel was not a man, she was very much a woman, and somehow he had to find a way to release the pent-up emotions which were silencing her tongue. But how?

Rachel was controlled again, and she glanced briefly into his face. "Will you take me back?" she asked again.

"Not yet," said Joel tautly. "Not yet." He forced his mind to go back over what had been said, trying to find the key to open the locked door. What had he said to arouse her to the extent that she had almost betrayed herself? What words had he used to create such an upheaval? What had they been talking about? Her husband? Gilmour? Yes. And – and the child . . . He tried to remember what he had said about the child. Was it his suggestion that she was marrying his father for the child's sake which had triggered her outburst? He had to try again.

Reaching for another cheroot, he said quietly: "And when

do you plan to get married?"

Rachel sighed impatiently. "I don't know exactly. In a few weeks."

"And until then you're going to go on living here?"

"I – perhaps."

Joel controlled his irritation. "And Sara? Will Sara live with you once you're married?"

She stared angrily at him. "Of course she will. Where else would she live? Oh, stop this, Joel, stop it now! I want to go back. I've been away long enough. Sara might waken –"

"I'm sure Hanson will be more than pleased to look after her for a while," returned Joel coldly. "She's not a baby, is she? What is she – three? Four? Old enough to understand when her mother isn't available."

Rachel drew an unsteady breath. "Are you going to take me back?" she repeated tremulously.

"And if I say no?"

"I can walk. I'm not helpless."

Her hand went to the door handle, but he forestalled her, reaching across her to prevent her from opening it. His arm was pressed against her breasts, and although she shrank away from his touch, he deliberately moved closer.

"What's the matter, Rachel?" he demanded mockingly, suddenly realising he had a far more potent weapon than force to arouse her. "If you're going to be my stepmama, what's wrong with us getting better acquainted? As I recall it, you used to like me to touch you."

She struggled to free herself, her breath coming in shallow gasps, and while mentally he could stand back and be appalled at the way he was behaving, something stronger than his self-respect was driving him on. Indeed, her nearness was having a most disturbing effect on him, and while love did not enter into his thoughts, lust was beginning to rear its ugly head. In spite of her slenderness, in spite of the severe hairstyle and unfashionable clothes, Rachel was still a very beautiful woman, and she had always had the power to disrupt his sensual processes, a power which he had once resented.

"Let go of me!" she stormed at him, her face twisted with contempt and bitterness. "I might have known it would come to this! This is all you're good for, isn't it, Joel!"

"What the hell do you mean by that?"

"It's the truth!" she choked. "You want everything and nothing, don't you? The body, without the mind. The pleasure without the pain?"

"What are you talking about?"

He was gripping her shoulders now, and while his brain told him he was achieving what he wanted to achieve, cold logic warned him that he might not like what he was about to hear. He shook her violently, and her hair came loose from the knot and fell in a silken curtain about her shoulders. She had never looked more abandoned, more desirable, and emotions, long dormant, returned to torment him. He was remembering the last time he had seen her like this, and then her needs had matched his own . . .

"Rachel . . ." he muttered hoarsely, but with a desperate effort she evaded his urgent mouth.

"Let me go, you brute!" she gasped. "Don't you dare to touch me!"

"Rachel, Rachel!" His fingers on her shoulders tightened. "You don't have to be afraid of me. My God, I loved you once. I'd never hurt you – "

"Wouldn't you?" She strained away from him, her face hectically flushed. "You don't expect me to believe that, do you?"

"Why, for God's sake?" Temper was hardening his voice. "What have I ever done to you? Tell me that. You walked out on me, remember? You're the one who split, who ran away without telling anyone where you were going! My God, I nearly went out of my mind! You're the one who quickly found some other man to take my place, so don't talk to me about hurting people!"

Rachel's lips curled. "You don't understand, do you, Joel? Even now, you haven't the first idea what I'm talking about." She shook her head almost pityingly. "Joel, Sara is not two or three years old. She's five. *Five!* Do you realise what that means?"

Joel's hands on her shoulders slackened, and his brows drew together causing deep lines to etch his forehead. An awful sick feeling was invading his stomach, and he was hardly aware of her staring at him, gauging his reactions, enjoying his shattering sense of horror and disbelief. Then his thoughts found coherence in denial.

"What are you saying?" he demanded thickly.

Rachel's triumph was short-lived, and she moved her shoulders helplessly. "I shouldn't have told you," she murmured dully.

"Shouldn't have told me? Shouldn't have told me what?" Joel was recovering fast. "Are you saying this child – this Sara – is my daughter?"

Rachel looked up at him almost defeatedly. "Whose else would she be?"

He moved his head confusedly. "Gilmour's, your husband's!"

"I had no husband, Joel. I've worked for Colonel Frenshaw for the past five years."

Joel almost flung her away from him, reaching grimly for the ignition key. "What are you doing?" Her white face was startled.

"What do you think I'm doing?" he retorted, breathing unevenly. "I'm taking you back to the Hall. I'm going to see my daughter – if she is my daughter!"

Rachel stayed his hand, gripping his arm tightly for a moment. "Oh, no," she said. "You can't do that– "

"Try and stop me!"

"I will. I'll do everything in my power to stop you," she declared. "I'll even go to the papers if I have to."

That momentarily stalled him, and he turned to look at her scornfully. "Why? Why shouldn't I see my daughter? Are you afraid for me to see her? Are you afraid I might find you out *in your lie?*"

"It's no lie." Rachel sighed. "Let me explain, Joel, just let me explain."

"What can you explain?"

Rachel shook her head. "Why do you want to see her? You don't like children, Joel. You always said so."

"But it seems I have one, doesn't it?"

"And you think that entitles you to call Sara your daughter?" Rachel was incredulous now. "My God, Joel, you've got a nerve!"

Joel raked his hands through his hair. He couldn't take in all this. He couldn't believe what had been said. It was some trick, some ploy on Rachel's part to make him squirm. It had to be.

Trying to remain calm, he said tautly: "All right. So I admit – children don't play any part in my life style. I'm a painter, Rachel, not a nursemaid!"

"Exactly."

"And do you think that opinion entitled you to keep my daughter's existence a secret all these years?"

Rachel plucked nervously at a strand of her hair. "Think back, Joel," she said jerkily. "Think back. Can you imagine what your reaction would have been six years ago, if I'd come to you then and told you I was expecting your child?"

Joel shifted restlessly. Six years ago he had still been making his way, six years ago ambition had been a driving force within him. It still was – but in a different way. And in any case...

"It should never have happened," he muttered. "You should have taken precautions – "

"*I* should have taken precautions? Oh, that's rich, Joel, that's really rich! *I* should have taken precautions. *I* should have made sure that because of your carelessness, nothing happened! Not you! Nothing should mar your pleasure! My God, Joel, you're a selfish swine! You are and always will be! Might I remind you that I had no way of knowing what you intended to do? I trusted you, Joel. I thought you loved me. I didn't know that sex was all you wanted all along – "

"That's not true, Rachel!" Joel was grim. "I loved you. I really loved you. And what happened – what happened – happened because we *both* wanted it to happen."

"*No!*" She put her hands over her ears again.

"Yes!" he muttered savagely. "I wanted to share my life with you, Rachel – "

"Share your life? Live with you, you mean!"

"Perhaps I did mean that initially," he conceded harshly. "But sooner or later – "

" – you'd have found someone else!"

"No, damn you. Sooner or later, I should have married you."

"How *gallant* of you!"

"Rachel, marriage wasn't among my plans at that time!"

"And children were among your plans at no time!"

Joel ran a hand round the back of his neck. He felt disorientated, confused. He didn't know what to think right now.

"Situations alter cases," he muttered.

"What does that mean?"

"It means that if – and I still say *if* – Sara is my daughter, I shall have to change my plans."

Her eyes widened incredulously. "What are you talking about?"

"We must get married, of course."

"Get married! *Get married!*" Rachel almost laughed in his face. "I wouldn't marry you if you were the last man on earth. My God, how conceited can any man be! Do you honestly suppose I'd marry you now?"

Joel grasped her forearms in a vice-like grip. "You don't have a lot of say in the matter," he snarled.

"Don't I? And what is your father going to say about this?"

For a second Joel had forgotten his reasons for being here. "I don't care what my father says," he retorted. "If the child is mine, she's mine."

"She's not a possession, you know, Joel. She's a person. A very special person in her own right. And those rights do not owe anything to you."

"What do you mean?"

"I mean that Sara is *my* child. You may have played some subsidiary role in her conception, but you can't prove that."

"Doesn't she look like me?"

Rachel's lips twisted. "Very much, as a matter of fact."

Joel's stomach muscles tightened in a most peculiar way. He found he desperately wanted to see this child – Sara.

"Then I should have quite a case," he said.

Rachel shook her head. "I'd deny it. I could always say she – she was – James's child."

Joel almost struck her then. The temptation was so great he had to thrust open the car door, and get out in the rain, taking great breaths of the cool, damp moorland air. That she should dare to taunt him with pretending the child was his own father's! It was some minutes before he dared to trust himself to get inside with her again.

When he did so, he was immeasurably calmer, but still as determined.

"I want to see my daughter," he stated steadily. "And one way or the other I intend to. Nothing you can say or do will stop me, Rachel."

Rachel was silent for several minutes, and then she said quietly: "What good will it do, Joel?"

Joel closed his eyes in agony for a moment, torn by emotions that threatened to overwhelm him. The past fifteen minutes had been the most subtle kind of mental torture, and his head ached abominably. What was she trying to do to him?

"You're a hard woman, Rachel," he muttered. "What happened to change you?"

"I think you know the answer to that!" she replied coldly. "Now, if you must – take me back!"

CHAPTER THREE

RACHEL got out of the car almost before it had stopped. She had been away from the Hall for over an hour and the thought that Sara might be awake and calling for her sent her hurrying anxiously towards the door.

"Wait!" Joel came striding after her, putting on his blue suede jacket, his face dark and withdrawn. "I'm coming with you."

Rachel halted awkwardly. "This is Colonel Frenshaw's house, Joel," she protested. "I can't invite you in without his permission."

"Oh, no?" Joel regarded her coldly. "Did you tell my father that, too?"

Rachel sighed. "Your father – knows Colonel Frenshaw."

"Ah, I see." Joel's mouth was sardonic. "A fellow-conspirator."

"Oh, don't be so ridiculous, Joel!" Rachel's nerves were stretched to screaming pitch. "I'll go – go and tell the Colonel you're here. I'll – ask him – "

"Don't bother." Joel passed her and opened the porch door. "Come on. You're not stalling me any longer."

Rachel gave him an angry look as she passed him, and then they were standing in the shadowy hall of the building, and the door was closed behind them. She didn't know what to do. The house seemed quiet, dead. She knew Colonel Frenshaw rested in the afternoons. Dared she risk taking Joel up to her suite of rooms without first telling him?

"Let's go!"

Joel was impatient and with reluctance she removed her coat and dropping it on to the chest in the hall, began to mount the staircase. Her rooms were on the first floor. This had been a major concession on the Colonel's part when it was first discovered that Sara had a tendency to run high fevers with what seemed to be only minor complaints. Before that, they had occupied rooms on the second floor, as did Hanson, the Colonel's secretary. She knew that initially Andrew Hanson had resented what appeared to him to be a show of favouritism, but when he realised the logic behind it, he had soon recovered. Rachel understood the jealousy he felt for his privileged position in the household, but she was not about to usurp that position. He had no cause for alarm. At that time nothing would have induced Rachel to consider marrying anyone. Now, it was different. It had to be different.

She was conscious of Joel following her, looking about him with interest. She felt she would never be able to repay the Colonel's kindness towards her, and that was why bringing a man, any man, into his house without his permission seemed a betrayal of his confidence in her.

She turned left at the first landing and walked to a door at the end of a hall. She entered an attractively furnished living room. Opening from this room were four other doors – her bedroom, Sara's, a small kitchenette and the bathroom.

Joel halted in the doorway to the living room, supporting himself against the jamb. "Cosy," he commented harshly. "Where is she?"

"She may still be sleeping!" retorted Rachel defensively, tense and distraught, dreading the moment when he must see the child for the first time. Sara was not a pretty little girl. She was too pale and angular, and if she took a dislike to someone as she had to Andrew Hanson, she could be most disagreeable.

But even as Rachel stood there, putting off the inevitable, Sara's bedroom door opened and Sara herself stood blinking in the aperture, her small jeans crumpled, her tee-shirt bearing evidence of the egg she had had at breakfast. Straight dark hair, painfully like Joel's own, hung to her thin shoulders, and her sallow cheeks and curiously dark eyes were unmistakably Kingdom in origin.

"Mummy?" she complained, looking frowningly towards the tall stranger lounging in the opposite doorway. "Mummy – you woke me!"

Rachel gathered herself, hardly daring to look at Joel. She had heard his swiftly indrawn breath when he first caught sight of his daughter, and his frown was a facsimile of Sara's. "I – I'm sorry, darling," she managed, going towards the child. "I – er – well, someone's come to see you."

"Who?" Sara's long lashes flickered. She sounded mutinous, and there was no welcoming smile to soften her sulky features.

Joel moved then. "Me," he stated ungrammatically, advancing into the room and closing the door behind him. "Me, your – er – " He halted as he glimpsed Rachel's horrified expression, and she had the feeling he was deliberately baiting her. "A friend of yours," he amended.

Sara looked suspiciously up at him. "I don't have any friends," she muttered uncompromisingly.

"Don't you?" Joel came down on his haunches beside her. "I'm sure you do." His face was almost on a level with her own. "What about – the Colonel – and Mr. Hanson?"

"I don't like Andrew!" retorted Sara rudely. "And the Colonel's too old!"

"Andrew?" probed Joel, and Rachel said: "Andrew Hanson," with some reluctance. "Ah, yes, I know." He didn't sound surprised. "And of course, there's no one else for you to play with, is there?"

"I don't play many games," stated Sara with childish candour. "I get tired. I'm a cripple, you see."

"*What!*" Joel straightened then, his eyes blazing in his dark angry face. "What does she mean?" he demanded. "What have you kept from me?"

Rachel shifted from one foot to the other. "N-Nothing. Nothing." She sighed. "I – Sara has a minor blood deficiency, that's all." *Oh, God forgive me*, she prayed silently. "It's being treated."

Joel looked unconvinced. "What's wrong with her blood?"

"I've told you, it's not important." Rachel looked down at Sara pointedly, and Joel compressed his lips. "Please, Joel, not now!"

"And who called you a cripple, Sara?" he asked at last, and the little girl looked anxious.

"Mummy?" she said questioningly.

"I expect it was the Colonel, Joel," interposed Rachel hastily. "Old people tend to say things . . ."

"No, it wasn't the Colonel," said Sara thoughtfully. "I heard them talking at the hospital. This man said: *Where is she?* and a woman said: *Who?* and this man said: *The little cripple*. I heard them."

"Oh, Sara, they might not have been talking about you," exclaimed Rachel, and Joel said: "What hospital, Sara?"

"The hospital in Whitstone," she answered. "I go every – "

"That will do, Sara," Rachel interrupted her, her face burning now. "Joel, don't you think you've said enough – "

"I want to know more about this!" he muttered, scowling, but she spread her hands.

"Joel, please. Don't make trouble, I beg of you!"

"What's the matter, Mummy?" Sara had sensed that the two adults were not sympathetic to one another and she scowled at Joel. "Why are you looking at Mummy like that?" she demanded fiercely. "Why did you come here? You're not my friend. You're only pretending. I don't even like you!"

"Sara!" Rachel was forced to put a restraining hand on the little girl's shoulder. "Sara, that was rude. Tell – tell Mr. Kingdom you're sorry at once."

"I don't have to!"

Shrugging off her mother's hand, Sara went across the room to where several dolls were upended in a small metal pram. Joel watched the child closely and Rachel found herself watching Joel, gauging his reactions. What did he think of her, this child who until today he had not even known existed? Did he find her unattractive? Was he disappointed that she was not a chubby pink and white creature, with doll-like eyes and curling hair? Yet Sara had so much more to offer – her loyalty and affection, her agile mind and undoubted intelligence, and most of all – that wealth of love which until now had been directed solely towards Rachel herself. For a moment Rachel allowed herself to wonder how Sara might react if she ever learned that Joel Kingdom was the father she believed dead. A grown-up Sara might find it unacceptable that Rachel had kept this fact from her over the years. Would she understand that because of what Joel had done, because of his irresponsibility her mother had found herself in the ignominious position of carrying a child inside her which its father would hate if he found out? Could she be expected to appreciate Rachel's fears at that time, or would the mature Sara feel sympathy in another direction? The idea was so unpalatable that Rachel could barely suppress the sob that rose inside her. She allowed her thoughts to go no further. She wanted nothing from Joel Kingdom, nothing at all. Not even for Sara's sake.

There was silence for several minutes and then Joel spoke. "This blood deficiency – how serious is it?"

Rachel turned away, rubbing her palms together. "I – I've told you. She'll get better."

"Has she seen a specialist?"

"She's seen several, as a matter of fact." She forced a shrug. "She's not unique. There will be other children exactly like her." That at least was the truth.

"But they're not my children!" Joel muttered harshly.

"Nor is Sara your child!" retorted Rachel huskily. "She's mine, and don't you forget it!"

"I don't forget anything." His voice was cold. "I have never forgotten anything to do with you!"

"Forgive me if I find that very hard to believe."

His jaw hardened. "Rachel, Sara is my child just as much as she is yours, and that's an inescapable fact! Your motives for keeping her identity a secret are your own, of course, but I doubt they'd stand a deal of questioning in a court of law!"

"A court of law!" Rachel turned on him then. "You dare to talk to me of courts of law! A great deal Sara has meant to you, hasn't she?" she hissed, and then glanced apprehensively at the child in case her words had carried across the space between them. But thankfully, Sara was engrossed with her toys.

"What was I supposed to do?" he asked grimly. "I'm not a mind-reader, Rachel." He glared at her. "I've told you already – how the hell was I supposed to guess that you might be pregnant?"

"You didn't care one way or the other!"

"You don't know that!"

"But you didn't want to marry me after – afterwards, did you, Joel?" she accused.

Joel's face darkened then as the warm colour rushed beneath the tan. "Rachel, if I had known –"

"Oh, yes. If you had known I was pregnant, things would have been different then, wouldn't they? What would you have suggested, I wonder? Adoption – or an abortion?"

Joel was taking a step towards her when the door of the living room suddenly opened and Andrew Hanson stood on the threshold.

"Rachel? I thought I heard voices – *oh!*" He saw Joel.

Rachel managed a faint smile. "Th-that's all right, Andrew," she assured him awkwardly. "I – er – Mr. Kingdom was just – going. He – he wanted to meet Sara, didn't you, Joel?"

Joel thrust his hands into his trousers pockets, his expression hostile. "I didn't know I was just *going*, Rachel. We haven't finished our – er – business yet, have we?"

Rachel's eyes implored his acquiescence, but Joel was not in a mood to accept it. Andrew Hanson's face mirrored his curiosity, but he manfully concealed it as he said: "I just thought I'd let you know, Rachel, the Colonel's awake and waiting for his tea."

"Oh, thank you." Rachel nodded her head jerkily. For the past few minutes she had almost forgotten the present in the disturbing reality of the past. She forced herself to look at Joel. "You'll have to go now, Joel. I – er – I have my work to attend to."

Joel looked at her, then at Andrew Hanson, and then round at Sara who was regarding all of them with the same degree of opposition. "I – er – I think I'll stay here with Sara," he said, much to her dismay. "You go ahead. Attend to your duties. I'll look after Sara."

"No, Mummy." Sara ran across the room to hide her face against Rachel's legs. "I don't want to stay here with him.I want to come with you."

Andrew Hanson frowned. "Don't distress yourself, Sara. No one's going to make you do anything you don't want to. Naturally Mr. Kingdom won't stay – "

"I suggest you mind your own business, Hanson," said Joel coldly. "This has nothing to do with you."

"Oh, Joel, *please*!"

Rachel tried to appeal to him, but Joel ignored her. "Will you leave us, Hanson, or do you want to be forcibly ejected?" he asked offensively, and the younger man turned and walked away, calling over his shoulder that he would see what the Colonel had to say about this.

"Oh, Joel!" Rachel stared at him across Sara's little body.

"What are you trying to prove? Go away. Go away now before you do any more damage."

"It's time you realised you can't bury your head in the sand any more, Rachel!" he bit out savagely. "My God, do you really think I'm going to leave it here? You still haven't told me why you're marrying my father. And I mean to know. There's more to this than convenience."

Rachel closed her eyes for a moment and then opened them again. "I don't have the time to discuss it with you, Joel."

"So what do I do? Stay in the village until you do?"

"No. No." She shook her head. "All right, if you must know, I'm moving to London next week. Your – your father has found me an apartment to stay in until – until we're married. He thinks it will be better for Sara. To see more of him. And – and afterwards – afterwards I suppose we'll be living a-abroad."

"Abroad!" Joel was astounded. "Where – abroad?"

"Your – your father has – has a house, doesn't he? On one of the Greek islands?"

"Lyarchos, yes. My God, you're not trying to tell me you're going to live there?" He shook his head. "What about the bank?"

Rachel shook her head. "That's not my affair. Our agree – that is – it was decided that it would be better for Sara –"

"So this has to do with Sara!" Joel smote his forehead with the palm of his hand. "Rachel, I won't let you do this –"

"You can't stop me!"

"I can try."

Sara was staring up at them now, her lips trembling as she felt the tingling violence of the interchange going on above her head. She stared resentfully at Joel, sensing this was all his fault, but not knowing how or why. Joel caught that stare and his lips twisted into the semblance of a smile.

"I'm going now, Sara," he told her mockingly. "But we'll meet again. Be assured of it."

"I don't like you!" Sara made a face at him.

"Now that's a pity, because I like you, I like you very much." His face hardened as he turned back to Rachel. "You'll be hearing from me!" he stated, and with a sardonic nod at both of them, he turned and left the room. Rachel heard his feet descending the stairs, the slamming of the outer door and presently the powerful roar of the Mercedes' engine.

Sara lifted her head as they heard the car drive away. "Is it going to be all right now?" she asked anxiously.

Rachel bent and hugged her, wishing she had someone to ask that question of and be reassured. "Of course it is, darling," she said gently. "And now I must go and get the Colonel his tea. Or I'll be in the soup!"

Ordinarily Sara would have questioned this, but today she was too absorbed with what she had just heard. "What did he mean, Mummy?" she asked worriedly. "Is it his daddy who's going to be my daddy? Will he be living with us as well?"

"Oh, no. No, darling."

"But he did say you were going to marry his father, didn't he? I heard him." Sara was distressed. She had heard enough of their conversation to know that everything was not exactly as it should be. They shouldn't have argued in front of her. But would anything have silenced Joel?

"Sara," she began, "the man – the man who was here just now is Mr. Kingdom's son, but he has his own home, his own apartment. He doesn't live with his father."

"Why not?"

"Well, because he doesn't. When people get grown up, really grown up, they get homes of their own."

"I shan't."

"Sara, you don't know what you'll do when you are grown up." *If she lived that long!* The unspoken thought smote Rachel with a pang. But she would grow up, she must, she told herself severely. Then, forcing a light tone, she added: "Girls usually meet someone and fall in love. Then they get married and have homes and children of their own."

"Like you did?"

Rachel hesitated. "Yes. Like I did."

"Oh, why did my daddy have to die?"

Rachel sighed. It was a long time since this subject had last come up and after the scene with Joel she was ill equipped to deal with her questions. "Darling, I have to get the Colonel's tea!"

"Well, anyway, I shan't do that," went on Sara imperturbably. "I shan't meet anyone and get married, I mean I shall stay with you for ever and ever and look after you."

Rachel's nerves were stretching by the minute. "That – that's nice, darling," she managed. "Now, I must get on. I've wasted enough time. Are you coming with me or do you want to stay here?"

"I'll come with you." Sara turned and went back to the pram. "I'll just get Helga. She likes watching you make tea, too."

Helga was a rag doll which Rachel had made three Christmasses ago. Old and scruffy now, usually without any clothes whatsoever, the doll nevertheless occupied a firm place in Sara's affections and went everywhere with her.

Rachel waited, cooling her impatience. She was glad she had something to do, something with which to occupy her mind. When she had started this she had known that sooner or later she was bound to meet Joel again, but she had not expected the encounter to be so bitter or so painful. It had been a gruelling couple of hours, a gruelling day really since Joel's appearance that morning, and her nerves felt shot to pieces. For the first time she wished that James Kingdom had been here to share it with her. Perhaps he knew of some way to control his son, but she did not.

It was late when Joel drove down the Bayswater Road and turned into Lancaster Mews. He had stopped at one of the motorway service areas and swallowed two whiskys and a packet of ham sandwiches because hunger and fatigue were beginning to affect his driving, and he wanted his wits about him when he got back to London.

His father's house was tall and white-painted and attractively Georgian in appearance. Its origins were doubtful, though, there being some talk of its having been a stables in years past, and James Kingdom had bought it after the conversion. There were servants' quarters on the ground floor, and the Talbots, a married couple who had been with his father as long as Joel could remember, had a comfortable flat there and coped with the cooking, housekeeping and chauffeuring between them. His father also owned a small estate in Wiltshire. That was where Joel had been brought up until he was old enough to go away to school. After that, his father had married again and Francis had been born, and things had changed. His father spent very little time in the country these days, but to be charitable Joel supposed that was because the bank occupied so much of his time.

He parked the car at the foot of the shallow steps which led up to the white panelled door with its significantly polished brass hinges. There were no lights anywhere in the building that he could see, but that did not mean his father had retired for the night. His study was at the back of the house overlooking a small walled garden, and it was here that James Kingdom spent most of his free time.

Joel had a key, and he inserted it carefully and turned the latch. The door gave inwards on to an attractively panelled hallway with the staircase to the main floor directly ahead of him. He closed the door and mounted the stairs two at a time. Immediately he was in the spacious living area of the building. This had been extensively modernised with lots of Swedish wood and leather furnishings. Joel switched on the lights and looked around. There was evidence of his father's occupation in the supper tray that still resided on a low table before the cowled hearth, but of James Kingdom himself there was no sign

Joel walked impatiently through a swing door into a half way. A light showed beneath a door at the end of the passage, and he strode towards it, opening his father's study door without preamble.

James Kingdom was seated behind his desk, working. Or at least Joel assumed he was working from the amount of papers strewn over the desk. His frown when he looked up cleared when he saw who it was who had interrupted him, and a sardonic smile slid over features that resembled Joel's own. They were alike, Joel accepted that, except that James Kingdom's face bore the imprint of his greater age and experience, and. his hair was quite white.

"Joel!" he exclaimed, getting to his feet. "This is an unexpected pleasure!"

Joel closed the study door and leant back against it, eyeing his father broodingly. "Don't give me that," he stated grimly. "You know why I'm here."

"Do I?" James Kingdom raised a heavy eyebrow.

"Without a doubt," essayed Joel, straightening to cross the room and pour himself some whisky from a decanter on a side table. He swallowed half the liquid in his glass at a gulp and turned back to his father, wiping his mouth with the back of his hand. "Without a doubt," he repeated.

James Kingdom subsided into his chair again. "Then would you mind pouring me one of those?" he enquired mildly. "It is my whisky, after all."

Joel's mouth twisted, but he complied, walking back to the desk with a glass and setting it down deliberately in the middle of the page his father was studying. "There you are! May I have another?"

His father looked up at him. "And if I say no?"

"I'm sure you won't," returned Joel mockingly, and walked away again.

But as he poured his second drink, Joel's face lost its mockery. This was no time for flippancy. His father was deliberately trying to sidetrack him.

"So?" James Kingdom sipped his drink with evident enjoyment. "To what do I owe the honour? It must be – let me see – the second visit during the last six months!"

"I lead a busy life," retorted Joel shortly.

"I'm sure you do. Not least because of the commissions I send you."

Joel's expression was ironic. "Oh, yes, I'll grant you that. Being the son of James Kingdom of the Kingdom Trust does have some advantages, obscure though they may seem. However, I would venture to suggest that it's my talent which keeps me in bread, not your name."

"And your grandmother's legacy!" inserted James dryly.

"That, too. Although in recent years I've reinvested most of it."

"Have you, indeed?" His father sounded impressed. "Being an artist must be more lucrative than I imagined."

"I'm a painter, Father, not an *artist*! When people think of artists they think of eccentrics in velvet caps and paint-daubed smocks!"

"Well, no one could accuse you of that!" remarked his father tersely, and Joel stiffened.

"Nor you either, so I gather."

"I wondered how long you'd take to get to the point of this meeting," observed James Kingdom, reaching for a cigar. "It's Rachel, of course."

"How did you guess?" Joel was sarcastic.

"I didn't have to, actually. Francis told me."

"I see." Joel swallowed the remains of his whisky. "How did you worm that out of him?"

"As a matter of fact, I wanted to see you. When you weren't available, I asked Francis if he knew where you were."

"And he told you? Just like that?" Joel was sceptical.

"No. He was most discreet. He said he thought you had gone away with Erica for a couple of days."

"And?"

"Erica answered her phone."

"Of course, you had to try it." Joel shook his head. "What did she say?"

"What you had told her, I suppose. That you had gone to Yorkshire on business."

"I see." Joel uttered a muffled oath. "Oh, you needn't go any further. I can guess what happened next. Francis isn't equipped to deal with your intimidation. Anyway, for God's sake, what does it matter how you found out? I saw Rachel and I saw *my* daughter!"

"Your daughter?" His father raised his eyebrows again.

"Yes. My daughter. And if you think I'm going to let you take her away from me, you're very much mistaken!"

"I don't think you have any say in it," returned his father mildly, and then drew back as Joel approached the desk. "And don't think you can intimidate me, son!"

Joel rested his palms on the desk. "You think not?"

His father sighed impatiently. "Oh, for heaven's sake, man, stop acting like a fool! All right, so you could physically overpower me. What good would that do? Do you think Rachel would appreciate such primitive tactics, is that it?"

"Let's keep Rachel's name out of this for the time being, shall we?'

"I don't see how we can. She's very much *in* it, isn't she?"

James Kingdom got to his feet then, as though the sight of his son towering over him was intimidating him, albeit against his will. "We're civilised human beings, Joel. Try and act that way."

"Is it civilised to expect me to accept my father marrying the woman who bore my child!" demanded Joel violently.

"You knew nothing about Rachel bearing your child, Joel, and don't you forget it!"

"You did, I suppose."

"As a matter of fact, yes."

"What!" Joel couldn't absorb what his father was saying. "What?" He came round the desk to his father's side and grasped his jacket grimly. "What did you say?"

James Kingdom shifted uncomfortably. "You heard what I said, Joel. I – I knew that Rachel was expecting your child."

Joel shook his head incredulously. Although he had heard the words, heard them in all their stark clarity, he couldn't believe it. His hold tightened and he glared at the older man with eyes that glittered dangerously. "What are you saying?" he ground out. "How could you know Rachel was pregnant? No one knew, except Rachel."

"I tell you I knew." His father tried to pull his jacket out of Joel's grasp. "Why is that so hard to believe? Rachel came to me. She was desperate. She asked for my help."

Joel's eyes were glittering threads of ice. "She – asked – for – your – help!" he echoed. "What could you do for her?"

"I could give her the money to get an abortion."

"An abortion!" Joel didn't seem able to stop himself from repeating everything his father said. "But – but–"

"– she didn't get an abortion," James finished abruptly. "She used the money to go away – up north. To keep her while she waited for the baby to be born."

"And you knew this?" Joel thrust his face forward and his expression was murderous.

"No! *No*!" His father shook his head vigorously. "I told you, I gave her the money to get an abortion. I didn't know that she hadn't."

Joel thrust him so violently away from him that James staggered against the bookshelves that lined the walls and only saved himself from falling by grasping the corner of his desk. But Joel wasn't watching him. He knew that he couldn't trust himself to touch his father without burying his fist in his stomach. He felt sick, violently sick, sicker now than at any time since he first heard that Rachel was involved with his father. That Rachel should have gone to his father and asked for money for an abortion! That she had deliberately avoided telling him, the one person she should have told!

Breathing deeply, he turned and looked at his father again. "Of course, it never occurred to you to tell me, did it?"

"Rachel begged me not to do so."

"Since when have you respected anyone's wishes?"

James sought the comfort of his leather chair, lowering himself into it slowly. Then he leant back and regarded his son sourly. "If the heroics are over, I suggest we discuss this matter in a sane and sensible fashion," he said harshly.

"How sane and sensible would you like me to be?"

"Joel, I wish you would keep out of this. It is between Rachel and myself – no one else."

"Not any longer. I want to know what gave you the right to pay Rachel to destroy my child?"

"You're being melodramatic, Joel!" James Kingdom brought his fist down hard on the desk. "For God's sake, man, Rachel was in desperate straits. You didn't want to marry her. Would you have had me turn her away?"

Joel came to the desk again. "You could have sent her to me. You could have *told* me!"

"Do you think she would have come? To you, I mean?" James shook his head.

"I think you didn't want her to." Joel's expression was contemptuous. "What an opportunity for you it was, wasn't it? What an opportunity to get back at me for all the occasions when I'd thwarted you, when I'd gone against your dictates!"

"You're talking rubbish!"

"Am I? Am I?" Joel sneered. "I don't think so."

"Doesn't it occur to you to wonder why Rachel never came to you herself?" James demanded angrily.

"No. She knew if she came to me, I wouldn't give her money for an abortion!"

"What would you have done?"

Joel hesitated, only briefly, but it was enough. "I – would have married her."

James stared at him derisively. "Would you? Would you? And do you honestly imagine Rachel would have married you under those circumstances? My God, Joel, you're arrogant! I sometimes wonder how I spawned you!"

"Flesh of your flesh, Father!"

"Be quiet!" James was incensed. "Rachel didn't come to you because she knew you for the selfish, ambitious swine that you are! You were ten years older than she was, but that didn't prevent your from taking your pleasure, from ruining her life –"

Joel turned away. "It wasn't like that!" he muttered violently. "I loved her –"

"*Love!*" His father snorted. "What word has been more abused? Love! You don't know the meaning of the word!"

Joel swung round on him. "And you do, I suppose? After two wives I suppose you feel you're pretty knowledgeable!"

James's face darkened. "I loved your mother, Joel, yes. No one could deny that. I idolised her. When she died . . ." He shook his head. "Francis's mother was different. Our marriage was never alleged to be a love match. We each lived our own lives –"

"– to the full!" Joel finished the sentence. "Oh, yes, I wasn't too young to understand what was going on, Father. All those house guests. You were no saint! You sit there prattling about selfishness and ambition! Weren't you selfish? Weren't you ambitious?"

"For you, Joel, only for you."

"For me!" Joel shook his head.

"It's true. You are my elder son, Joel, the son of the woman I worshipped and adored. Was it unnatural for me to want to mould you –"

"In your image, yes!" Joel paced impatiently about the floor. "For heaven's sake, Father, this is getting us precisely nowhere. I didn't come here to talk about the past, except insofar as it impinges upon the future. You've sidetracked long enough. I want to know how you came to find Rachel again – how you came to ask her to marry you. And more important why she is doing so. I know it's to do with the child, with – Sara." He said his daughter's name slowly, experimentally almost. Then he shook his head. "What's wrong with her? Why does she attend hospital? And why do they call her a cripple?"

James Kingdom squashed out the remains of his cigar. "Didn't you ask Rachel these questions?"

"Damn you, I'm asking you them!"

His father shrugged. "I'm afraid that if she didn't relieve your curiosity, I can't either."

"Father, I warn you – "

"No." His father got to his feet again. "*I* warn *you*, Joel. Keep out of this! For years now, you've treated this house with contempt, you've never come here, I've never seen you. You haven't given a damn about my health and welfare. Well, until now, that situation hasn't been to my liking. But now it is. Now

I want you to stay away, spend your time with the people you seem to care about. I know it must be galling for you to accept that Rachel might conceivably prefer me to you, but that's something you're going to have to live with – "

"You don't care about Rachel – "

"On the contrary, I'm very fond of her. I like her very much. I always did. Even in the days when you poisoned her mind against me."

"With good reason, you must admit," muttered Joel bitterly.

"Perhaps. I admit, I haven't always been this benevolent. But times change."

"Times might, you don't." Joel could feel a throbbing in his temples. Slowly but surely, this was getting through to him, and the impotency of his position was tearing him to pieces. But why? Why? He had got over Rachel years ago. All he felt for her now was a blind resentment that she should have walked out on him, have kept this from him. "What have you told her about me?"

James shrugged. "Hard as it must be for you to accept, Joel, we seldom discuss you at all. Rachel's had a pretty rough time these last few years. I intend to make things easier for her."

"By marrying her?" Joel raked his hand through his hair. "You could make things easier for her without marrying her."

"What?" His father's smile was derisive now, and Joel felt close to choking him. "And leave the field open for you, Joel?" he scoffed. "Oh, no. The little agreement Rachel and I have made is only binding on the marriage contract."

Joel drove back to his apartment overlooking Regent's Park with a pounding headache. He had left his father's house before his control snapped altogether. He felt sick, and empty inside, and more angry than he would have believed possible.

He tried to gauge how he would have felt if it had turned out that Rachel had really been married to someone else if Sara had been the imaginary Gilmour's child, and couldn't. It was impossible for him to separate the two things in his mind, but when he considered his father's proposed marriage he didn't think of the child, and his imagination painted pictures more vivid than any he had created on canvas. His recollections of his affair with Rachel had never been more acute, and the ache in his loins was a real and physical thing...

He drove the car into the underground parking area and took the lift up to the penthouse floor. When he entered the apartment, he was startled to find a lamp still burning in the huge living area, and a young woman sleeping on the burgundy velvet couch. The sound of him closing the door disturbed her however, and she lifted her head with a welcoming smile.

"Joel! *Darling!*" she exclaimed, stretching rounded white arms. "I thought you were never coming!"

Joel came down the two shallow steps that led into the main body of the room, unbuttoning his jacket as he did so. "What are you doing here, Erica?" he asked shortly, tension tautening every line of his features.

Erica Grey lifted delicately arched brows. "Hardly the welcome I was expecting, darling," she chided him gently. "I gather your business in Yorkshire didn't go as well as you expected."

Joel passed her and went to the drinks trolley standing against the wall, helping himself to a stiff whisky and swallowing it before saying: "Did Heron let you in?"

"Yes. Four hours ago," she conceded dryly. "Joel, what is it? What's wrong? Aren't you pleased to see me?"

She slid off the couch and stood before him, slim and assured in her dusky pink chiffon gown. Chestnut dark hair curled fashionably about her small head, and her heels added inches to her diminutive five feet of height. Rachel was much taller, he found himself thinking, and then brushed the thought angrily aside.

"I'm sorry, Erica," he sighed. "I'm very tired, that's all. And I've got a filthy headache. I want nothing so much as a shower and bed!"

"Oh, darling!" She came towards him then, her hands outstretched, and pretended not to notice when he moved away. "Can I get you something?" she asked, linking her fingers together. "An aspirin – or some seltzer?"

Joel shook his head. "No. No, nothing, thanks." He ran a hand over his forehead. "I'm sorry, I'm not much company, I'm afraid."

Erica's tongue probed her upper lip. She had sensed his uncertain mood, and she knew from experience that a careless word could ignite a furnace.

"I'll go," she said, reaching for the fur cape she had draped over the back of the couch on her arrival. "I'll ring you tomorrow, shall I?"

Joel regarded her impatiently. He despised himself for treating her so casually, but right now he was in no mood to be tactful. It was easy to excuse himself on the grounds that she shouldn't have been here, but on other occasions – after a particularly demanding lecture, or a boring evening spent as the guest of one society or another – he had been glad of her sympathetic companionship. Erica demanded little of him; she was independent and reasonably intelligent, and as his mistress she was always available. He knew that eventually she expected him to marry her, but this had never troubled him. The demands of her own profession offset his, and having children played no part in her scheme of things, which had suited him. She was not cut out to be a mother, she had told him; she was shrewd and sophisticated, intent on making a success of her career, and this was what he had thought he wanted. But suddenly the selfishness of that kind of life revolted him, and all he could see were two stormy dark eyes glaring up at him in obvious dislike. It was insane, but those eyes haunted him. And yet was it insane to want your own daughter to at least *like* you?

But he could explain none of this to Erica, and she was left to draw her own conclusions as to his unsociability. She draped the fur over her shoulder and walked to the door, and with a genuine effort, Joel followed her.

"Yes, ring me tomorrow," he said, bending to kiss her lightly, and finding himself withdrawing from that avid seeking mouth. "Goodnight, Erica."

"Goodnight."

Erica's smile was tinged with impatience now, but she managed to restrain the impulse to rail at him for his indifference. Joel closed the door after her with real relief, leaning back against it and closing his eyes. He had known exactly what Erica was thinking, but he had been unable to reassure her.

Straightening, he crossed the living room, loosening his tie and dropping his jacket where it fell. A short passage beyond an attractively arched doorway brought him to his bedroom, and he went inside wearily and closed the door behind him. A shower, in the cream and gold luxury of his bathroom, did much to destroy the feeling of contamination he had experienced after the row with his father, and wrapping a towel around his hips he went back into his bedroom. Shaded lamps cast spotlights of colour on chocolate brown walls, and the massive four-poster bed was spread with a coffee and cream printed quilt. Joel sat down on the edge of the bed and then lay back to stretch his arms behind his head. He was tired, exhausted – but it was not just a physical thing. He was tired of painting portraits of society women, who, without conceit, he knew lived in hopes that he might desire more of them than his statutory fee; he was tired of receptions and parties, and more food and drink than was good for him; he was tired of prostituting his soul for the benefit of his body; in short – he was tired of his life.

CHAPTER FOUR

SARA was finally asleep, and Rachel tiptoed silently out of the bedroom and closed the door. It had taken some time to settle the child down, she was disturbed and excited by her new surroundings, by everything that had happened to her that day, and her temperature had risen alarmingly. But now, at last, she was sleeping soundly and Rachel breathed a sigh of relief as she walked back to where James Kingdom was awa˙ -ing her in the living room.

This flat, one in a medium rise block in a cul-de-sac off Abbey Road, was much bigger than she had expected. Apart from the comfortable living room, there was a kitchen big enough for herself and Sara to eat in, two bedrooms and a bathroom. It was a furnished flat, but far more luxuriously furnished than anything Rachel had ever occupied, and she realised that James had gone to a great deal of trouble on her behalf. It should, she supposed, have made her feel more grateful to him, but their relationship was still so new and alien to her that her gratitude was diluted with a certain amount of cynicism. Nevertheless, the flat was near to St. Matthew's Hospital, and that was the important thing. When the time came for Sara to enter hospital, Rachel would be able to visit her whenever she wanted.

James Kingdom was seated on the long couch when she re-entered the living room, but he rose at her entrance and indicated the seat beside him. "Come and sit down," he said. "Let me get you a drink. What would you like? Gin – whisky – vodka?"

"Just a dry Martini, please," replied Rachel, sitting down on the edge of an armchair, and with a wry smile he walked across to a polished cabinet which opened at the touch of a switch to reveal a comprehensive array of bottles and glasses.

When he returned to his earlier position on the couch, he was carrying two glasses, and handing one to her, he commented: "You look tired too, Rachel. I shan't keep you long. I expect you'd like an early night."

Rachel sipped her drink slowly, nodding. "It has been rather a hectic day," she conceded. Then, realising something more was expected of her, she added: "It was kind of you to meet us at the station and take us out for a meal. Sara loved it."

"It was only what I wanted to do," replied James, lying back in his seat, watching her closely. "I guessed you wouldn't feel like preparing food today. By the way, the cupboards in the kitchen are well stocked. My secretary saw to all that."

"Thank you." Rachel didn't know what else to say.

James's face mirrored his satisfaction at the situation as it now stood. Even in a plain tweed skirt and a rather shapeless sweater, Rachel had style and elegance, but he was determined to mould her into the kind of woman people would expect his wife to be. Claudine, Francis's mother, had had style. Probably still had. But she had been indiscreet, and a divorce had had to be arranged.

"I've arranged for you to visit the Grey Salon some time this week, Rachel," he remarked casually.

"The grey salon?" Rachel looked up in surprise. "What is that?"

"The Grey Salon, my dear! It's a rather exclusive dress shop, owned by a friend of Joel's, as a matter of fact."

Rachel could feel the colour creeping up under her skin. "Oh!" she managed blankly.

"Yes. Erica Grey. No doubt when she finds out who you are, she'll attend to you herself."

"What do you mean?" Rachel couldn't prevent the instinctive defence

"Why, only that you're my fiancée, my dear," returned James smoothly. "What did you think I meant? I haven't broadcast it around among my friends that my fiancée was once my son's mistress!"

Rachel got jerkily to her feet, spilling her drink on to the warm red carpet. "That's a foul thing to say!" she choked.

"I agree." James sounded apologetic. "I'm sorry, I shouldn't have said it."

"I was not – his mistress," stated Rachel tremulously.

"No. No, I know." James sighed, shaking his head. "Forgive me?"

Rachel stared down blindly into her glass, and then she moved her head in a positive gesture. James relaxed. Then: "I'm afraid I was trying to hurt you – as you've hurt me by withholding the knowledge that you've seen Joel since our last meeting!"

Rachel felt rather like a fly must feel in the web of a rather disingenuous spider. She had known she should have mentioned the incidence of Joel's visit, but the memory of it was still too raw to bear examination.

"How – how did you find out?" she ventured.

James sighed. "Joel told me."

"Joel?" Her eyes widened.

"Yes. Did you think he wouldn't?"

What had she thought? She didn't know. Perhaps she had imagined that Joel would avoid an open confrontation with his father. She should have known better.

"He – he came to the Hall just over a week ago," she told him in a low voice. "The Colonel didn't see him. He – he demanded to see Sara."

"And you told him whose child she was, didn't you?"

"Yes." Rachel drew a deep breath.

"Why? Because of Sara's resemblance to her father?"

"I – no." Her clenched fingers tightened about the glass. It would be so easy to say that was so. To lie about it. But lies led to more lies and that was no beginning for a relationship. "He – he hadn't seen Sara when I told him."

James's heavy brows arched above the bridge of his nose. "Then why did you do so?"

Rachel moved away from him, shaking her head. "Oh, it was terrible. We had a row – an awful row. I suppose I wanted to shock him with the truth. I succeeded."

"And were you not going to tell me about this? Didn't you think that I ought to know? To be forewarned, as they say?"

Rachel shrugged. "I – there hasn't been a lot of time . . ."

"No." James inclined his head. "I suppose there hasn't." His eyes narrowed. "Of course, Sara doesn't know of her relationship to my son?"

"No!"

"That's good. I don't want us to have secrets from one another, Rachel. Don't forget, without my help you would have no recourse but to appeal to Joel. Is that what you want?"

"Of course not." Rachel's mouth trembled. "You know I could never do that."

James made a dismissing gesture. "So. We'll say no more about it. It's tomorrow morning that you have the appointment to see Lorrimer, isn't it?"

"Yes. Yes. Ten o'clock."

"Are you nervous?"

Rachel hesitated. "Are you?"

James gave the question his consideration. "Apprehensive, perhaps," he mused. "But Lorrimer is, without doubt, the most able man in his field. There's no cause for alarm."

"But if it fails – " Rachel began unsteadily.

"– then Sara will resume her present treatment." James looked at her encouragingly. "Nothing ventured, nothing gained. I'm sorry if I'm speaking in clichés, Rachel, but you really must be more optimistic."

Rachel finished the Martini and cradling the glass between her palms, said: "I will."

James studied her for a few minutes longer and then bent his head to kiss her lips. But Rachel jerked aside and his mouth slid harmlessly along her cheek. He straightened then and his eyes were hard as they probed hers. "We have a bargain Rachel," he stated coldly. "I trust you. Don't you trust me?"

Rachel compressed her lips. "Oh, yes, of course I do, James. But don't rush me. It's been an exhausting day. Can't you appreciate that?"

James nodded, and his expression softened slightly. "Of course. I was forgetting." He swallowed the remains of his drink and set the empty glass on the mantelshelf. "I'll go, then you can get to bed. But I'll be round to see you tomorrow evening before I leave for Frankfurt. I'm sorry I have to go away the minute you arrive in London, but this may be my last conference."

Rachel managed a faint smile and accompanied him to the door. When he bent to kiss her again, she accepted his kiss dutifully, and if he noticed that there was no enthusiasm behind it, he made no demur.

After he had gone, Rachel carried the dirty glasses into the kitchen and rinsed them at the sink. It was an attractive kitchen with lots of orange paintwork and chromium handles. When she opened the cupboards she found an impressive array of china and glassware, and food to feed a garrison. There were fresh fruit and vegetables, milk and butter in the refrigerator, and a french loaf in the bread bin. Someone had catered for them very adequately.

It was half past nine by the time she re-entered the living room, and weariness was a leaden weight on her shoulders. But the thought of entering her lonely bedroom just yet filled her with dismay and she deliberately switched on the television and tried to pay attention to the play that was in progress. But her thoughts kept wandering, and when it finished and the news came on she had not been aware of what she had seen.

It was strange to think of the Hall being closed and shuttered now. It had been their home, hers and Sara's, for the past five years, and Colonel Frenshaw had been as much a friend as an employer. An invalid himself, engrossed in writing his war memoirs, he had welcomed a young person about the place, and when Sara was old enough to toddle about and chatter to him, he had been delighted. Indeed, Rachel didn't know how she would have coped without the Colonel's assistance...

But the Colonel's health had deteriorated rapidly over the past twelve months, and he had been advised to seek a warmer, drier climate, if it was at all possible. He had wanted Rachel to go with him, he had assured her that he would make the necessary arrangements for Sara, but Rachel had been loath to accept. She owed the Colonel enough already, and besides, sooner or later she would have to make other arrangements. Far better to make them here, in her own country, as attempt to make herself understood to some alien official who might not be sympathetic without the Colonel's support behind her.

It had been an oddly fortuitous twist of fate that had brought James Kingdom to Langthwaite. She had known the Colonel had dealings with a bank in London and that its chairman was someone the Colonel had known well when he himself had lived in London just after the war. When the Colonel had first decided to sell up and move abroad, it had been natural that he should contact his old friend about his securities, and James Kingdom himself had decided to attend to the matter.

Rachel shivered. She could still remember the wave of horror which had swept over her when she opened the door to James Kingdom. He had recognised her at once, and although she had not told him about Sara, the Colonel was only too willing to discuss his attractive housekeeper, who had lost her husband before her baby was born.

James had lost no time in putting two and two together and coming up with the right answer. He had found an opportunity to talk to Rachel, and question her about her disappearance, and although Rachel had not particularly wanted to talk to him, as the guest of her employer she could hardly refuse. She had decided to tell him the truth, and although she had been apprehensive about doing so, James had been curiously sympathetic. Especially when he learned of Sara's disability.

That was when he had first broached the possibility of a bargain being struck between them. He wanted a wife, he said. He had a notion to retire, but it would be a lonely existence without a woman's companionship, and if Rachel wanted security as well as recovery for Sara, she would do well to consider what he had suggested.

And Rachel had considered it. She had considered it late into the night, night after night. At first, the idea of marrying James Kingdom had been anathema to her, but gradually the benefits to Sara which would ensue had stilled her other fears She owed it to Sara to do everything in her power, not only to make her well again, but to ensure that Sara would never be faced with the struggle for survival Rachel herself had once faced. After all, James was the child's grandfather. He must have some natural feeling for her. And they would live most of the year in Greece, he said, and if all went well Sara would eventually return to England and attend a good school there. She would have every advantage that money could bring, advantages Rachel could only guess at after spending her formative years in an orphanage, and she would never need to work unless she really wanted to do so. How could Rachel turn it down?

Of course, she hadn't. She had eventually agreed that if the tests James was to have made proved positive, she would marry him on his terms. The tests were extensive and Rachel lived on a knife edge. But eventually he came to her with the news that this thing he had suggested was possible.

Getting up, Rachel switched off the television and went into her bedroom. There was a connecting door with Sara's room and earlier she had left this ajar. Now she went to the aperture and listened intently. Sara was breathing easily, apparently recovered from her experiences of the day. Rachel bit her lower lip hard. What if something disastrous happened? she asked herself desperately. What if the operation went wrong and Sara died? Would she ever be able to forgive herself?

Surprisingly, Rachel found she slept quite soundly, and awakened to the unaccustomed hum of traffic from the main thoroughfare some yards away from the apartment building. A watery March sun was filtering through the curtains and she wondered rather optimistically whether she should regard it as a good omen. She could hear sounds from the room next door and a smile curved her lips. Sara was obviously exploring her domain and had charitably not decided to wake her.

Sliding out of bed, and pulling on her navy quilted dressing gown, Rachel went to the door into Sara's room. The little girl was busily unpacking her canvas holdall, in which she had stuffed all her favourite toys, into the bedside cabinet. She looked up when Rachel spoke to her, and smiled broadly.

"You're a sleepyhead!" she said, blinking. "I've been awake for hours!"

Rachel glanced automatically at her watch and then relaxed when she saw it was only half past eight. "Did you sleep well, poppet?"

"Mmm. It's a lovely bed." Sara bounced up and down upon it as though to demonstrate its elasticity. "Will I have a bedroom like this when we go to live with – with that man?" Although James had asked her to call him "uncle", Sara didn't seem capable of doing so, and she invariably said "that man" which jarred on Rachel.

"I expect you'll find living abroad quite a novelty," she replied, briefly. Then: "Now, go and get washed while I sort out the clothes you're wearing to go to hospital."

Sara slid off the bed and then hesitated doubtfully. "I – I don't have to stay in hospital today, do I?" she asked anxiously.

"No." Rachel shook her head. "Today you're only going to see Mr. Lorrimer. You remember Mr. Lorrimer, don't you? You met him the last time we were in London."

"When we stayed at that big hotel?" Sara's eyes were round.

"That's right." Rachel half smiled. "Now, go along. Get washed."

The telephone rang as they were having breakfast and Rachel felt her nerves tighten as she lifted the receiver. But it was only James Kingdom's secretary ringing to ask whether there was anything else they required. Rachel assured her that there was not and thanked her for taking so much trouble on their behalf.

"That's all right, Mrs. Gilmour, it's my job," the secretary replied politely, but Rachel sensed that she didn't altogether approve of the situation.

After breakfast they walked to the hospital. St Matthew's was not a new building, but it had been recently modernised and its facilities were as comprehensive as those found in many strictly larger establishments. Fortunately, Sara was used to her attendances at hospital in Whitstone, and apart from showing a natural curiosity about her new surroundings she did not seem nervous. Rachel was more nervous than she was, but then she had more cause. She knew exactly what they were entering into.

Mr. Lorrimer, the surgeon in charge of Sara's case, was a man in his early forties, of medium height and build, who nevertheless possessed a certain presence that inspired confidence in his patients. He was particularly responsive to children, Rachel had learned this on their previous visit, and although Sara had only met him once, she allowed him to examine her without demur. Because he had seen her before, the examination did not take long, and afterwards Rachel helped the doctor with the necessary documentation while Sara played with Helga. Arrangements were also made for Sara to attend the hospital for her treatment, and by the time it was over Rachel felt infinitely more relaxed.

James Kingdom came to the apartment again that evening. Sara had had her supper and was all ready for bed when the ring came at the bell, and she scampered to answer it while Rachel hastily tidied the strands of hair that had come loose into the chignon at her nape. Sara was disposed to talk about their visit to the hospital, and about her liking for Mr. Lorrimer, and Rachel was relieved that the child's presence obviated an immediate *tête-à-tête*. Nevertheless, eventually Sara had to go to bed, and when Rachel rejoined her guest in the living room, he was looking well pleased with himself.

"You see," he said, when he had settled her in an armchair with a drink, "already Sara is at home here. It's not going to be so difficult, is it?"

Perhaps not so far as Sara was concerned, thought Rachel, wryly, but she said: "Children soon adapt. That's one of the advantages of being young."

James clicked his tongue reprovingly. "You talk as though you were middle-aged!" he exclaimed. "Just because I'm some years older, don't pretend that you're not young, too. I like your youth, Rachel. It's one of the many enchanting things about you. Who knows, we may yet have children of our own."

Rachel stiffened. She couldn't help herself. "Oh, I don't know – " she began awkwardly, but James wasn't listening to her.

"I shall be away approximately ten days," he was saying, and she dragged her thoughts back to him. "That should be time enough for Sara to get used to her new surroundings, not only here but at the hospital, and when I come back . . ." He shrugged. "We can talk about that later. Be assured, all the necessary arrangements are made."

"I know," Rachel nodded. "Mr. Lorrimer told me."

"Good. And he'll keep you informed all along the line. You have confidence in him, don't you?"

"Oh, yes." Rachel looked down into her glass. "And – and when it's over . . ."

"Greece is an ideal place for recuperation."

"But – the Bank . . ."

"Francis is not a fool, my dear, and Geoffrey Morrison can manage."

"But for how long? James, you know you told me –"

"I told you that I'd hoped Joel would follow in my footsteps. This is true. Unfortunately, Joel has rejected all claims to his inheritance. Nevertheless, all is not lost. Francis will have to do for now. At least his name is Kingdom. But, if all goes well, I may yet have a son I can mould in my image."

His eyes glinted, and it was impossible not to understand what he was saying. He would not have the slightest qualms about disinheriting Francis if it suited him to do so. He was quite ruthless in business; this she had learned from Joel years ago . . . But it was quite impossible to imagine herself the mother of any child of his . . .

"By the way," James emptied his glass and regarded her thoughtfully, "I've made arrangements for Mrs. Talbot to come round here and stay with you while Sara is in hospital."

"Mrs. Talbot?" Rachel frowned. "Oh – your housekeeper?" She shook her head. "That's not necessary."

"I disagree. I don't like the idea of you staying here alone when I'm not around to take care of you."

"You mean – when you're in hospital, too?"

"And while I'm away."

"But Sara's only in the hospital overnight."

"Nevertheless, I would prefer to know you were not alone."

He was adamant, and short of having an argument with him there was nothing Rachel could say. But she couldn't help wondering whether his concern for her welfare had anything to do with Joel.

The next morning, before James left for Frankfurt, he rang Rachel from the airport.

"I forgot to tell you, my dear," he said, "Miss Clay will be calling for you this morning to take you to that dress salon I was telling you about." Miss Clay was his secretary.

"But I don't need any more clothes," protested Rachel.

"Let me be the judge of that." James paused. "Rachel, much as I admire your appearance, as my fiancée you must understand you will be in the public eye. Allow me to dress you as a member of the Kingdom family should be dressed."

"I'm not a member of the Kingdom family yet, James."

"You soon will be, Rachel. Humour me! I shall look forward to the transformation on my return."

Rachel had made no definite promise when she rang off. As usual, there was little point in trying to explain that she would prefer to remain independent until they were married. But if Miss Clay was going to insist on taking her to the Grey Salon, what little money she had would soon be swallowed up if she attempted to buy her own clothes.

Lydia Clay was a woman in her late forties who had worked for the Kingdom organisation since she was a young girl. The fact that she was now secretary to the chairman revealed a certain singularity of purpose. Looking at her immaculately made up face and city-smart navy suit, Rachel couldn't help wondering whether she had never entertained any feelings for her undoubtedly attractive boss. Rachel had sensed the woman's disapproval of her relationship with James Kingdom from the first occasion she had visited the office, and could only assume she found the disparity in their ages totally incompatible.

Lydia had arrived in a taxi to take them shopping, and it was waiting downstairs when they left the building. The Grey Salon was in a narrow alleyway off Regent Street, and from outside had little to commend it. But once within the swing glass doors, once stepping across the soft grey carpet, one was immediately aware of a hushed air of expectancy that intrigued the buyer. Rose-pink chiffon drapes concealed all but what one was allowed to see, and there were none of the racks of suits and dresses Rachel was used to flicking through. Sara, small and somewhat incongruous in these surroundings, in her jeans and anorak with Helga dangling from her hand as usual, looked about her with interest. Then she said, with childish candour: "The shop's empty, Mummy. Have they sold out?"

Even Miss Clay's lips twitched at this, but a sales assistant was crossing the floor, and she controlled herself sufficiently to say: "Good morning."

"Oh – good morning, Miss Clay." The assistant evidently knew her, and Rachel wondered whether it was on her own account, or whether part of the reason for Miss Clay's antipathy was that she had done this sort of thing before.

"We'd like to see Miss Grey," went on the secretary smoothly. "Is she available?"

"As a matter of fact, she is," replied the assistant, her gaze flickering rather wryly over Rachel's plain pants and vinyl jacket. "If you'll come this way . . ."

They passed through the chiffon drapes into an inner salon. The carpet here deepened to charcoal, and there were chairs and cubicles, and a small dais for modelling. The assistant saw them seated, and then went away to find her employer.

Rachel felt tense. She was remembering what James had said about this Miss Grey being a friend of Joel's. What kind of a friend, and how close a friend, was she? And when she saw

Sara, would she raise her eyebrows as Miss Clay had done? Or would there be some stronger reaction?

Rachel had expected someone of Junoesque proportions, but Erica Grey was tiny. Elegant, in a slim fitting grey suit, her darkish hair a mass of curls, she made Rachel feel tall and ungainly, and the swift appraisal she made of Rachel's clothes was denigrating.

"So you are Mrs. Gilmour," she greeted her coolly. "Mr. Kingdom told me you were coming. How do you do? I'm Erica Grey."

Rachel shook hands. "How do you do?"

Erica's cool surveillance took in Miss Clay, and then alighted on Sara. "This is – your daughter, Mrs. Gilmour?"

Sara wrinkled her nose, and half hid herself behind her mother's legs, and Rachel nodded. "That's right. This is Sara."

Erica's thinly moulded lips curved downwards. "How do you do, Sara?"

The child made no reply, staring at them mutinously, and a slight frown marred Erica's smooth brow. Clearly, the Kingdom resemblance was striking her too, and thankfully Rachel remembered that James was a Kingdom himself.

"She's not very like you, Mrs. Gilmour, is she?" Erica suggested, veiled insolence giving an edge to her voice.

Rachel summoned all her small store of confidence. "No, Miss Grey, she's not. Actually, she very much resembles her grandfather!" And let her make what she likes of that, she thought childishly.

Whatever Erica Grey's personality might lack, her clothes sense was impeccable, as Rachel soon learned. The casual slacks and sweater she had worn to come in were stripped away, and their place was substituted by well-fitting suits and dresses in strong colours that accentuated Rachel's fair colouring. But her skin was not the normal skin of a blonde, its pigmentation was darker, and tanned easily in strong sunlight. Consequently it was apt to look sallow in pastel shades. Erica, however, discarded anything that she felt did not blend well with the image she wished to create, and Rachel emerged as a slender young woman who while needing a little more flesh on her bones, had nonetheless the ideal figure for high-waisted, longer skirts, flared trousers, and floating drifts of chiffon lace. Carried away by the artistry involved, Erica paid little attention to the protests Rachel voiced from time to time, simply assuring her that she had had her orders from Mr. Kingdom, and it was up to her to carry them out.

Miss Clay sat through the proceedings saying little, and ignoring Sara completely. For a while Sara was patient, sitting in her chair, enchanted by the transformation being wrought upon her mother, but as the minutes stretched into an hour, and one hour into two, she began to get restless and kept asking how much longer they were going to be.

Rachel would have liked to have been able to tell her, but in Erica Grey's hands she was given no opportunity to do so. Besides, it was so long since she had taken any trouble with her appearance, other than making sure she was neat and clean, that she, almost against her will, found herself enjoying the experience.

And then, as she emerged from one of the cubicles wearing a long sapphire blue velvet gown, with a low tight-fitting bodice and long sleeves that fitted her upper arms closely before belling out in mediaeval fashion from her elbows, she heard a male voice in the outer salon, and before she had time to gather herself, a man strode through the draperies and confronted them. It was Joel, and at once Erica left what she was doing to go and greet him.

"Darling!" she exclaimed warmly, reaching up to touch his cheek with her lips. "What are you doing here?"

Joel looked over Erica's head at Rachel and the look in his eyes brought the hot colour to her cheeks.

"Oh, I – er – I just thought I would come and take a look at my – stepmother-to-be!" he remarked mockingly.

CHAPTER FIVE

THE only person who showed no surprise at Joel's words was Erica. But then Erica was already dressing Rachel on James Kingdom's instructions, and so far as she was concerned, the situation was a *fait accompli*. But Miss Clay looked disapproving, Sara was scowling, and Rachel . . . Well, Rachel thought, as she strove for composure, his words had been intended to shock her, and they had succeeded.

Joel turned from Erica to Sara, and bending down beside the child, he said: "And what do you think of Mummy's new clothes?"

Sara wrinkled her nose and pursed her lips and stared at him and he grinned, surprisingly, wiping several years off his age. "That's a pretty face," he commented dryly. "Now pull an ugly one!"

Sara pursed her lips even tighter, but something about his grin made them wobble. "Go away. I don't like you," she declared, when she could no longer sustain the grimace, and Miss Clay clicked her tongue reprovingly.

"Sara!"

Rachel spoke for the first time, and Joel looked up at her in insolent appraisal. "Well, well. You *shall* go to the ball, Cinderella," he mocked, and her face suffused with colour. But in this instance, he did not wait to see the results of his offensive, but turned back to the child. "Aren't you bored sitting here watching the fashion show?" he asked, taking hold of Helga's free hand. "I know a place where they sell strawberries topped with ice cream and nuts and chocolate sauce. Wouldn't you rather come with me to see what we can find until Mummy's finished?"

Sara jerked Helga away from him. "No."

"Are you sure?" he persisted. "They sell iced lollies, too – "

"I don't like iced lollies!" retorted Sara, but she didn't sound at all convincing.

"Stop trying to bribe her, Joel," burst out Rachel then, aware that Erica was regarding him in some amazement. "Sit down, Sara. We won't be much longer, and then I'll buy you an ice cream."

Sara ignored what Rachel had said to move nearer to her mother's skirts. But she didn't take her eyes off Joel, who straightened and hooking his thumbs into the low belt of the corded pants he was wearing, said: "Now who's bribing her?"

"Sara doesn't want to go with you, Joel," said Rachel shortly. "I should have thought that was obvious."

"Would you?" He switched his attention to Sara. "Is it obvious, Sara? Wouldn't you like to come for a ride in my car? And I'd like to draw a picture of you."

"A picture of me?"

Sara's eyes were wide and Rachel felt furious. "Joel, please," she exclaimed, but he ignored her.

"Yes, Sara. A picture of you. Like this one."

He drew a folded sheet of sketching paper out of his pocket and beckoning her to come closer, he opened it up. Sara hesitated a moment, looking up appealingly at her mother, begging her approval, but Rachel couldn't give it. She was far too finely drawn. She didn't know what Joel's game was, what he was trying to do, to *prove*, but she despised him for using Sara in this way.

Sara, however, was unaware of any undercurrents. Her initial antipathy was fading beneath a natural curiosity, and when she ventured to take a look at the paper he held in his hand, she gave an excited cry: "Why, it's me! Isn't it? *It's me!*"

"Mmm, mm." Joel nodded indulgently. "Do you like it?"

Sara snatched the paper out of his hand and darted back to her mother, exhibiting the charcoal sketch of her head and shoulders which Joel must have drawn from memory, with great pride. The sketch, like all Joel's work, was excellent. A clear impression of how she had appeared to him, straight from sleep, that day at the Hall. Rachel's stomach muscles tautened nauseously, and it took an immense effort of will power to nod and say: "It's – it's very good, darling."

Sara took the sketch again, turning it this way and that, admiring her image. "My hair looks nice, doesn't it?" she asked, of no one in particular. "But I wish I'd been smiling."

"You didn't smile at me," commented Joel wryly, and she looked up at him steadily, almost assessingly.

"If I let you draw me again, will you make me smile?" she demanded, and Rachel said: "Sara! Mr. Kingdom is a busy man. I'm sure he has better things to do than draw little girls."

Her eyes challenged Joel's, but were not equal to the task. "On the contrary," he contradicted her, "I'd like nothing better than to draw Sara again. That is, if she'll come and have that ice cream with me. I hate eating ice cream alone."

Sara chewed thoughtfully on her lower lip, and Erica said: "I thought you told me you were lecturing this morning, Joel!" in rather terse tones.

Joel shrugged. "I decided to give it a miss. I – er – I didn't feel like lecturing today. Not to students, at least."

Erica made an impatient gesture. "Don't be facetious!" She glanced irritably at the child. "I'm quite sure you didn't come here just to invite Sara for an ice cream."

Joel narrowed his eyes. "Why, Erica, would you like an ice cream, too?" he mocked, and she turned away in disgust.

Sara had turned her attention to Rachel. She was clearly torn between the desire to do what her mother obviously wanted her to do and the attractive temptation not only of enjoying a delicious ice cream sundae, but also having her picture sketched.

"Mummy?" she murmured doubtfully. "Mummy, would you be awf'ly cross if I went with – with Mr. Kingdom?"

Rachel avoided Joel's gaze. "Is that what you want to do?" she asked jerkily.

"Well, only a little while," admitted Sara reluctantly. "I wouldn't be long, really I wouldn't. Would I?" She looked up at Joel.

"You can be as long as you like," replied Joel, shrugging his shoulders. He forced Rachel to meet his stare. "I know where you live. If you're going back there after you're finished here, I'll fetch her home in time for lunch, hmm?"

Rachel was in an impossible position and both of them knew it. "Oh, very well then," she muttered with ill grace. "And – and Sara!" This as Sara took a couple of skips across the soft carpet. "Sara, behave yourself. And – and no gossiping!"

Sara knew what this meant. She understood that she hadn't to talk about her illness. Instead, she smiled, and Rachel looking at her realised that no one could doubt her ancestry. It was there in every quirk of her eyebrows every quiver of her mouth, every look that teased and challenged and tore at her heart. Joel offered his hand, and Sara took it, and they went out together, but after they had gone the atmosphere was distinctly strained.

"I didn't know Joel knew your daughter so well," commented Erica, tugging viciously at the zip of the velvet gown.

Rachel stepped out of it and shook her head. "He – he doesn't. That is – he's only met her once before," she said hastily.

"And yet he can sketch her from memory?" Erica sounded sceptical. "I wouldn't have thought she was so unforgettable."

Rachel refused to answer this, and the other girl went on: "Of course, she'll be his stepsister when you marry James

Kingdom, won't she?" Her lips twisted. "And looking at her, one can see that the relationship is not misplaced."

Rachel took a deep breath. "I think I've seen enough clothes for today, Miss Grey," she stated, with apparent calmness, although she was anything but calm inside. "If you would just send me the almond green suit and the purple dress and jacket – "

"My instructions were to provide you with a wardrobe, Mrs Gilmour. I'm sure you would not wish me to offend Mr. Kingdom by doing less than he is paying me for."

Rachel looked at Erica, then at Miss Clay's wooden face, and then back at Erica again. What was the use in getting all steamed up with them when it was Joel who was responsible for everything that had happened He had only done it to hurt her, and if Erica's relationship with him was as warm as the other girl would have them believe, she had every right to exhibit a show of natural pique.

Looking round for the sweater and slacks she had worn to come in, she said: "Do what you think is best, but if you don't mind, I've had enough for this morning."

There was a pregnant silence, and then Erica seemed to pull herself together. "I'll have all the suitable garments adjusted where necessary and sent round to Mr. Kingdom's house, shall I?"

Rachel shook her head, still searching for her clothes. "No. I have a flat. I'll give you the address. You'd better send the things there."

"Very well, Mrs. Gilmour." Erica was coolly polite again.

"Do you know where my slacks and sweater are?" asked Rachel frustratedly.

Erica cast a bleak look around. Then she shrugged and said: "I would suggest you wore something a little more – elegant, shall we say, for town?"

Rachel held her cold gaze for several seconds, and then turned away. "Thank you. But, I'd prefer to wear my own clothes as long as possible."

The assistant, who had earlier hovered about with pins, putting tucks into garments and shortening hems, soon uncovered Rachel's belongings and she quickly dressed, stifled suddenly by the atmosphere in the salon. As she and Miss Clay bade Erica goodbye and walked outside, Rachel couldn't help the uncharitable thought that James had sent her here deliberately, knowing that sooner or later she would learn of Erica's association with Joel. It was the kind of thing he would do – like confronting her with his knowledge of Joel's visit to Langthwaite, when she was least expecting it. She wondered if he speared flies on pins. Perhaps he imagined she still harboured some feelings for Joel. She did – but they were not the kind of feelings that need trouble him.

Leaving Miss Clay to take a taxi back to her office, Rachel walked idly along Regent Street, looking in shop windows. It was strange being alone in the city. It reminded her of her student days, the days before she knew Joel...

She stopped and stared determinedly in a travel agent's window, but the display was meaningless to her. Why was it that every thought she had, every memory she possessed, sooner or later came back to Joel Kingdom? She had had a life before she met him; why couldn't she think about that?

But she had not had a very happy childhood. Orphaned before she was old enough to remember her parents, with no aunts or other relatives to take care of her, she had been brought up in a children's home where love naturally came second to the ordinary practicalities of living. She had made friends there, of course, and there had been happy times; but it wasn't until she was old enough to break out on her own that she began to feel like other girls of her age. A student grant enabled her to find a room in a boarding house, and she had attended the Maxwell College of Design and Craft. She had always had an eye for colour, and her designs at the grammar school she had attended had been so good that she had been recommended to take up a career in commercial art. She had been at the College for about nine months when Joel Kingdom came to lecture to the students.

He had noticed Rachel at once, probably because of the silky curtain of silvery hair which at that time had fallen about her shoulders, she conceded now, and when he had wanted a model to demonstrate his use of colour, he had of course chosen her.

To begin with she had refused to have anything to do with him outside of the college, and although the other girls all thought she was mad she had been adamant. But one night he had been waiting for her outside the college, and as it was pouring with rain she had allowed him to give her a lift home. After that he was there every evening, and sometimes she allowed him to take her to dinner. She realised now that she had been foolish to imagine she could fool around with a man like Joel Kingdom without getting her fingers burned, but then everything had seemed so simple.

Joel could be the most charming man imaginable, and before long, almost without her being aware of it, she had fallen in love with him. Even then, she had not felt the first tremors of apprehension. Joel had told her he loved her, too, and although she was aware that for the present he had no intention of getting married, she imagined that when that happy event did occur, she would be his wife.

How stupidly naïve she had been, she thought now, her hands balling into fists in her pockets. Marriage had never been on Joel's agenda, at least, not marriage with someone of her background, and his opinions concerning children should have given her fair warning. He had talked a lot in those days about people he knew whose lives had been stunted by their children. He had said he didn't believe that everyone naturally felt the urge to replace themselves, and he pitied couples who had had to sacrifice their youth to bring up their families, who, as soon as they were old enough, left to live lives of their own. Rachel had pretended to agree with him, secretly harbouring the belief that his own mother's death when he was only a few months old was responsible for the callousness he displayed. He had never known a mother's love, but when they were married he would want children just as much as she did.

She began to spend a lot of time at his apartment. She got to know his man, Heron, and began to feel at home there. Joel was working quite exhaustingly at that time, and very often she was alone in the lounge reading, while he worked in his studio. She brought her work to the apartment, and occasionally benefited from his expert advice. On other occasions, they would just sit together, listening to records or simply talking, and Rachel had never been happier or more content. But it didn't last...

Joel suffered from migraine. The attacks were not frequent enough to interfere too drastically with his demands upon himself, but one evening, an evening when Heron had been given the night off, Rachel arrived at the apartment to find him pale and sweating, frantically trying to finish a painting for an exhibition to be held two days later. She had persuaded him that he was a fool to go on, that he could not possibly do his best work in that condition, and that he must go to bed and relax, give in to the pain and let it run its course.

Eventually he had agreed to do so on the condition that she should stay with him, stay in the apartment and not go home until he could take her. Rachel had been doubtful, but finally persuaded by his unexpected weakness, and she had left him to rest while she remained in the lounge.

She must have fallen asleep on the couch because she awakened in the early hours of the morning to find Joel bending over her, his migraine apparently improved and a disturbingly sensuous expression in his dark eyes.

She had never forgiven him, or herself, for what had happened. But it had been inevitable. Newly awakened, soft and yielding from sleep, utterly responsive to Joel's demanding passion, she would have been inhuman to remain immune to his lovemaking. Besides, she had loved him, she had wanted him just as much as he had wanted her, and when he had lifted her up into his arms and carried her into his bedroom, it had all seemed so right. Not at all the sordid thing it had become later . . .

The next day she had discovered exactly how important it had been to Joel. Far from apologising for what had happened, he had seemed to regard it as the natural progression of their relationship with no mention of marriage to justify his loss of control.

Rachel had been shattered, hopelessly disillusioned, furious with herself for behaving so recklessly. She had despised Joel for using her as no doubt he had used other women in the past, and devastated that their association should apparently mean so little to him . . .

After avoiding him for over a week, during which time she had suffered a series of phone calls which deteriorated from urgent appeal to angry abuse at her continued prevarication, she had agreed to meet him and confront him with her feelings. It had been a terrible interview. Joel had begun by pleading with her, and ended by telling her that he was not yet prepared to sacrifice his freedom for the sake of her propriety. He had told her to be sensible, adult, to grow up; to accept that these days virgins were out of date. All he had done, he had taunted her, was to put her in the fashion.

They had said a lot of hurtful and cruel things to one another, things which afterwards Rachel bitterly regretted. It had been an undignified way to conduct an argument. And even then she had known that Joel did not really believe she was through with him. He still wanted her, she knew that, but he had destroyed any feeling she had had for him.

And then, three weeks later, she had discovered that there was another penalty she was going to be made to pay for that reckless night. She was pregnant, without money, and utterly determined never to ask Joel for anything ever again . . .

Realising that the sales assistants in the travel agents were beginning to stare at her with equal intensity, Rachel pulled herself together and moved away. She wondered where Joel had taken Sara and whether she was enjoying herself. A bitter pain stirred in her breast. That would be ironic, she thought without humour. If Sara became attached to her "step-brother". What would James Kingdom have to say about that?

It was just after twelve o'clock when Rachel arrived back at the flat, but there was no sign of the cream Mercedes which Joel had been driving the day he had come to Langthwaite. She let herself into the apartment, and taking off her jacket went to make herself some coffee, as much for something to do as anything. The percolator was bubbling when the doorbell rang, and trying to calm herself she went to answer it.

Sara bounced into the flat, Helga in one hand, waving a sheet of sketching paper in the other, babbling about what they had done and where they had been, but for once Rachel's eyes didn't immediately move after the child. They were drawn, almost against her will, to the narrowed gaze of the man who had halted mockingly in the doorway, regarding her with enigmatic intent.

"Safe and sound, as you see," he commented, leaning against the doorpost. "Are you going to invite me in?"

Her concentration split by Sara tugging at her hand, wanting to show her what she had brought, Rachel said unsteadily: "Is there any reason why I should?"

"None. But equally, there's no reason why you should not,"

returned Joel crisply, and straightening he came into the living room

Rachel was forced to give all her attention to the child then, taking the sketch Sara was offering, feeling her heart skip a beat as she looked at the image Joel had created. His talent had never been in any doubt, she had admired his work for a long time, the facility he had for getting into his subject and producing the essence, as well as the likeness, of his craft, but Sara's portrait was different somehow. She told herself it was her own closeness to the subject, her awareness of Sara's vulnerability which gave it its brilliance, but it was more than that. If she had not known better, she would have said that there was real feeling behind every line. But what kind of feeling she could not hazard to guess.

"See – I'm smiling," pointed out Sara with satisfaction, and Joel snorted humorously.

"That's because of that enormous sundae you swallowed," he commented, flinging himself uninvited on to the couch and stretching his arms above his head. "I bet you'll be sick later."

"I bet I won't." Sara left her mother to walk towards the couch. "Anyway, you had one, too."

"Not as big as yours."

"You could have one." Sara was practical. Then she hugged Helga closely. "It was lovely, though. Does that man really do all your cooking?"

Rachel's head jerked up and she thrust the sketch onto the nearby table. "What man? Where have you been, Sara?"

"We went to Joel's house – high up, ever so high up in the sky! We went up in this lift that went – "

"You took her to your apartment!" Rachel was horrified.

Joel turned hard eyes in her direction. "Why not? You've been there plenty of times."

Sara's eyes widened. "Have you? Have you really, Mummy? Have you seen all the houses – "

"Yes, yes!"

Rachel was abrupt, but she couldn't help it. She realised only too well that Joel was showing her how easily he could destroy her and she hated him for it. And had he told the child to call him by his Christian name?

"Your mummy and I were – friends, years ago," he was saying to Sara now. "That was – before you were born."

"Did you know my daddy?"

Sara was excited, but Rachel had had enough. "Of course he didn't." she broke in tersely. "Sara, it's almost lunchtime. Say goodbye to – Mr. Kingdom, and go and wash your hands. I'm going to open a tin of soup, and it will be ready in five minutes."

Sara looked disappointed, and for a minute Rachel thought she was going to be awkward. But then, after exchanging a glance with Joel, she seemed to think better of it, and scuffing her feet made her way towards the door.

"G'bye, Joel," she said, holding on to the handle, and Joel smiled and said: "Be seeing you, Sara."

After she had gone, Rachel looked down at him coldly. "I – I suppose I have to thank you for – for looking after Sara," she said reluctantly.

"Not if you don't want to." Joel got to his feet and now she had to look up at him. "I enjoyed it. She's an intelligent child. I found her company – stimulating." He paused. "I want to see her again."

"You can't!" The words were uttered before Rachel could think better of them. Then, seeing the hardening of his features, she tried to reason with him: "Joel – please! Be sensible! There's no point in making things worse."

"Is it unreasonable for me to want to get to know my own daughter?" he demanded harshly, tall and darkly menacing before her. The heavy silk shirt he was wearing was half open down his chest revealing the brown column of his throat, he wore a cream denim jacket and navy corded pants that moulded his lean hips and exposed the muscles of his thighs, and he was so close she could smell the heat of his body. "Don't you think you owe me a little of her time?"

"I owe you nothing!" retorted Rachel, twisting her hands together, despising the sudden remembrance of the feel of his hair-roughened skin against her flesh that the male scent of him had evoked. "You *take* what you want, don't you, Joel? You don't *ask* for anything."

"No, but you do," he muttered violently, his hands on her hips jerking her towards him, and before she could protest, his mouth had descended on hers.

Rachel had a fleeting impression that his action had taken him by surprise as much as her, but from the moment her lips parted under his all her energies were taken up with trying to resist the devastating weakness that surged over her. His hands moved over her back, arching her body towards him, making her familiarly aware of the hardening angles of his. Lethargy was swamping reason, his mouth was moving on hers, probing and seeking. Her fingers spread themselves over his chest, and she was filled with the crazy desire to put her arms around his neck and twine her fingers in the thick strength of his hair.

"Mummy?"

Sara's curious little cry brought Rachel to her senses, and with a groan of dismay she dragged herself away from Joel and went towards the child, checking her hair with trembling fingers, pulling her sweater down over her hips.

"So there you are, darling," she managed jerkily. "H-have you washed your hands?"

Sara pursed her lips and stared sulkily beyond her mother to where Joel was raking his hair, taking deep steadying breaths "What were you doing when I came in?" she asked.

Rachel cast a curious glance over her shoulder at Joel. Then she made a casual gesture. "Sara, you don't understand – "

"I was kissing your mother!" stated Joel, without prevarication. "Haven't you seen two people kiss before?"

Sara's troubled expression eased a little. "Why were you kissing Mummy?"

Joel shrugged his broad shoulders. "You may well ask," he muttered, his tone coldly ironic. "Look, I've got to go." He walked towards the door ignoring Rachel's resentful stare. "I'll be seeing you soon, Sara. Goodbye, Rachel."

Rachel said nothing. She did not trust herself to speak. The way she felt right now she could have flown at him and scratched his eyes. out. How typical, she thought bitterly. How typical of his behaviour. That he should create the situation and then walk away and leave her to pick up the pieces!

The door closed behind him and Sara transferred her attention to her mother. "I don't think that man – Joel's daddy – would like you to be kissing Joel," she stated with her usual perspicacity. "I don't like you kissing him either. You're my mummy, not his."

"Oh, Sara!"

Rachel gathered her daughter into her arms and hugged her closely. If only it was that simple, she thought despairingly. If only the jealousy of a child was all she had to contend with . . .

CHAPTER SIX

THE following evening, Sara was to go into hospital for her treatment. She would be staying in overnight as usual, but Rachel had decided not to contact Mrs. Talbot, in spite of what James Kingdom had said. Apart from anything else, she hardly knew the woman, and just at the moment she felt ill prepared to deal with strangers.

During the morning, a messenger arrived from the Salon, loaded down with the boxes of clothes and footwear and lingerie, which Erica Grey had considered necessary to equip the woman who was to be James Kingdom's wife. At least Sara had a delightful time opening all the packages and pulling out the dresses, parading around Rachel's bedroom with one or another of them draped in front of her. Rachel supposed she should have stopped her, but quite honestly the idea of a man, *any* man, buying her clothes was anathema to her.

Eventually she pulled herself together sufficiently to hang all the dresses and suits in the fitted wardrobes, and Sara carefully arranged the shoes and sandals on a rack. There were blouses and cashmere sweaters which Rachel was sure she had never seen before, and she could only assume that Erica had sent these to demonstrate that she took her instructions from James Kingdom only.

Nevertheless, Rachel would not have been human if she had not found some of the things very attractive, and deciding that ignoring the inevitable would get her precisely nowhere she changed from her own slacks and sweater into a pair of close-fitting corded velvet jeans in a rather unusual shade of green, and a vivid purple blouse made of some soft synthetic fibre.

The transformation was satisfying. The well-fitting pants accentuated the slender length of her legs and the rich colour of the blouse made a perfect foil for the silvery lightness of her hair. It was amazing, she thought cynically, what clothes could do. Already she looked years younger and less obviously thin.

In the afternoon, she and Sara decided to go sightseeing. Sara had never seen the Houses of Parliament or Buckingham Palace, and with the spring sunshine glinting through the trees it was pleasant to walk in St. James's Park and feed the ducks on the lake. Rachel talked to Sara about her life in London when she had been a student, and Sara said she would like to be a student one day. And she would be, Rachel told herself fiercely. If she could go through with this...

When they arrived back at the flat, however, there was a rather unpleasant surprise waiting for them. Mrs. Talbot, James Kingdom's housekeeper, was there, and from the polished state of the furniture and the lunch dishes which Rachel had left in the sink draining on the board, she had not been idle while they had been out. Rachel felt an angry sense of frustration that James should have given this woman a key to her flat. It made a mockery of his ringing the doorbell and waiting to be admitted.

Mrs. Talbot smiled half apologetically as they came in. "Good afternoon, Mrs. Gilmour," she greeted her politely. "Hello, Sara." She smoothed her hands down over the blue checked overall she was wearing. "I hope you don't mind, Mrs. Gilmour, but I've just been tidying round a bit for you."

Rachel hesitated, biting her tongue. Then, controlling a sharper retort, she said: "How did you get in here, Mrs. Talbot?"

The housekeeper shrugged her shoulders. "Mr. Kingdom left me a key, Mrs. Gilmour. He thought you might be going out quite a lot, and he asked me to keep an eye on the housework."

"Did he? Did he really?"

Rachel unfastened the soft camel coat she was wearing, another of James's purchases, and taking it off flung it over the back of a chair. She realised that Mrs. Talbot wasn't to blame for the situation, but that didn't make it any easier to take.

Turning to Sara, she began to help her off with her anorak, and Mrs. Talbot spoke again. "I – er – I've got the kettle on, Mrs. Gilmour. Would you like a cup of tea?"

Rachel straightened, folding the anorak between her hands. Then she sighed resignedly. "Why not?"

Sara looked curiously at her mother as Mrs. Talbot went to make the tea. "Why is she here?" she asked.

Rachel forced a smile. "Oh, Mrs. Talbot has just come to help Mummy with the housework, that's all. Run along and wash your hands. I expect you'd like a biscuit and some milk, wouldn't you?"

Sara nodded and trotted off to the bathroom while Rachel summoned her reserves of composure and went to find Mrs. Talbot. The older woman was in the process of pouring hot water into the teapot, and a faint colour in her cheeks indicated that she liked this situation no more than Rachel.

"Look," said Rachel quietly, "I'm sorry if I was offhand just now. But I didn't know if James had a key to the flat. I should have known better."

Mrs. Talbot finished pouring the water and put the kettle down. "That's all right, Mrs. Gilmour," she said, putting the teapot lid into place. "I guessed you weren't aware of Mr. Kingdom's arrangements. But he said he had told you that I was to sleep here while Sara was in hospital overnight."

Rachel breathed deeply. "I see." Now she was beginning to understand. "But how did you know that Sara was going into hospital this evening?"

"Mr. Kingdom checked with St. Matthew's before he left, Mrs. Gilmour."

"Of course, he would." Rachel nodded. "Oh - well." She shrugged. "I suppose we'll have to make the best of it."

Mrs. Talbot looked slightly relieved. "If you'll show me where I'm to sleep, Mrs. Gilmour, I'll go to my room and leave you in peace."

"Oh, don't be silly." Rachel shook her head now. "I should feel grateful for - for James's concern." Her lips twisted. "Naturally you'll eat with us, and I'm sure you'd rather watch television than sit in your bedroom all night."

Mrs. Talbot smiled then. "That I would. But you don't have to entertain me. If you'd like to go out - visit friends . . ."

Rachel turned away so that the older woman should not see her face. "I - er - I have no friends in London, Mrs. Talbot," she said.

The telephone rang as Rachel was helping Sara to put a few of her belongings into the canvas holdall she always took with her when she went into hospital. Mrs. Talbot was in the living room, so she answered it, and she came to the door of Sara's bedroom looking rather surprised.

"It's Mr. Joel Kingdom, Mrs. Gilmour," she informed her politely. "Will you go and speak to him?"

Rachel's face flamed, but she couldn't help it. When the phone had rung, she had assumed it would be either James or his secretary, and she had been prepared to tell him that she didn't care for his methods. But what on earth could Joel want? Had he found out that Sara was spending the night in hospital? Had he discovered the real reason behind her marriage to James?

All these thoughts flashed through her mind and it was difficult to get to her feet and behave as though there was nothing peculiar about her future husband's son telephoning her. But Mrs. Talbot was almost bound to mention the call to her employer, and while the housekeeper was unaware of

Rachel's previous association with Joel, she could not help but speculate upon his reasons for contacting her in his father's absence. As for James himself . . .

Leaving Mrs. Talbot with Sara, Rachel walked quickly into the living room and picked up the waiting receiver. "Yes?"

Her voice betrayed her anxiety, and Joel said: "I'm sorry. I didn't know you had a watchdog."

Rachel ignored his mockery. "What do you want, Joel?"

"I want to talk to you, Rachel. I was going to suggest coming round there after Sara was in bed, but obviously that's out of the question now." He paused. "However, as you do appear to have a built-in baby-sitter, perhaps we could have dinner together."

"No, thank you, Joel."

He uttered an expletive. "You can't dismiss me like that, Rachel. One way or another, we're going to talk. If you want me to come round there . . ."

"You know you can't!" Rachel was desperate.

"All right, I accept that. So what do you suggest?"

"I – I can't suggest anything." Rachel cast a worried glance over her shoulder. If Mrs. Talbot should overhear any of this . . . "Joel, couldn't you phone me tomorrow?"

"Why? Will the watchdog have gone by then?"

"Mrs. Talbot will be leaving in the morning."

"It seems a wasted opportunity."

"I – I can't see you tonight!"

"If you insist." He was silent for a moment. Then: "I'll take you both out for lunch tomorrow. I know somewhere we can go where Sara won't prove too much of a distraction."

"I don't know, Joel – "

"Eleven-thirty, Rachel," he stated uncompromisingly. "I'll call for you." And he rang off.

Rachel replaced her receiver carefully and stood staring, down at the cream instrument for several seconds. And then

with a sigh, she went back to Sara's bedroom.

Leaving Sara at the hospital was always a wrench, and particularly so this time when all the nurses were strangers to her. She looked so small and helpless in the high hospital bed, the machine that had kept her alive for the past six months feeding on her like some monstrous vampire. And yet that was an unfair analogy. It was Sara who took her life blood from the machine.

Afterwards Rachel walked back to the flat slowly. She was reluctant to join Mrs. Talbot, reluctant to have to discuss Sara's condition with anyone at this time. She felt she needed an escape for a while from the tortuous probings of her own thoughts, and wished she had a car that she might drive out of town and away from the flat which reminded her so acutely of her involvement with James Kingdom.

Ever since the previous afternoon she had felt restless and uneasy, and Joel's call this evening had not helped matters. What did he hope to achieve by harassing her like this? What were his intentions? And what could he have to say to her that had not already been said? If he imagined his unprovoked attack on her senses had aroused anything but disgust inside her, he was mistaken, yet every time she remembered those moments in his arms a *frisson* of something akin to fear swept over her. Perhaps it was this that troubled her most. Joel was – he always had been – a man of strong sexual attraction, and the possibility that he might be using that attraction to gain his own ends filled her with alarm. She half wished James had not had to go to Frankfurt. Right now she felt very much alone.

She was approaching the cul-de-sac where her flat was situated when a low dark green sports saloon came by her and then unexpectedly stopped just ahead. Rachel slowed her pace, alarmed as to the driver's intentions, and then surprised as the nearside window was rolled down and she found herself looking into Erica Grey's unsmiling features. But Erica was not alone, nor was she the driver of the expensive vehicle, and when the driver's door was thrust open and a man climbed out, Rachel was not surprised to find it was Joel Kingdom. He came round the car towards her, and his face was grim and uncompromising.

"What the hell are you doing wandering about the streets at this time of night?" he demanded curtly, dark and attractive in a maroon velvet dinner suit, and for a moment Rachel was taken aback.

"It's not late," she said defensively, and then, as her composure returned, "It's none of your business."

Aware that Erica could hear every word they said, Joel's only reaction to this was a distinct thinning of his mouth, but his eyes promised retribution later. "Get in the car," he said. "We'll take you home."

"Thank you, but I only have a few yards to go," replied Rachel tautly, and realising that Erica must be feeling furious at this intrusion, continued: "It was a – fine evening, and I felt like a walk. I'm used to doing a lot of walking. Good night." Her eyes flickered over Erica. "Goodnight, Miss Grey."

"Wait." Joel's fingers curved round her upper arm, preventing her from moving. He was closer now, and Rachell could feel her heart pounding in her ears. Her fingers brushed the soft material of his jacket as she endeavoured to free herself, and his eyes, unblinking and compelling, bored into hers. "Have you eaten?"

Rachel managed to nod her head. "Yes. Yes, of course." She dragged her eyes away from his face. "Can I go now?"

Joel's fingers tightened deliberately round her arm, biting into the flesh, sending waves of pain to her fingertips. Then with a grimace of self-derision, he let her go and walked back to the car. "We'll wait until you turn into the apartment building," he remarked, and with a feeling of humiliation

Rachel hurried round the corner into the cul-de-sac and into the block where her flat was situated.

She was stupidly near to tears and she told herself it was because of his deliberate cruelty, but the inner agony she felt was more than a physical pain. She wondered what Erica Grey must have thought of his behaviour, but knew well enough that such anxieties would not trouble Joel. He believed he could get away with practically anything, she told herself bitterly, and he probably could. Even so, she had been shocked by his conduct, and she wondered if there was anything significant about his being around at this time of night. Casual encounters were not always the result of chance.

Drawing a steadying breath, she began to climb the stairs to the flat. There was a lift, but she was glad of the exercise. It would provide an excuse for her flushed cheeks and quickened breathing.

It was as well that she had returned to the apartment as she had. Only a few minutes after she got in, the telephone rang, and this time it was James Kingdom.

"I guessed you wouldn't long be in," he said, his voice sounding as if he were in another room, not another country. "Did Sara settle down at the hospital?"

"Yes. Very well." All the resentment Rachel had been feeling before Joel's call and her subsequent encounter with him seeming petty and unimportant now. "How are you?"

"Oh, I'm fine. Very busy, of course, but very well. Did Mrs. Talbot turn up as I asked her to do?"

Rachel's eyes flickered over the back of Mrs. Talbot's head as she watched the programme on the television at the other end of the room. This was her opportunity, but she couldn't take it. "I – yes. Yes, she's here."

"That's good. I don't like to think of you staying in the flat alone."

"Sara's hardly a bodyguard," remarked Rachel dryly. But

perhaps she was – in James's book. It depended what one wanted to guard.

"I know," James was saying now. "But I thought you might worry about her more if you were alone."

That was reasonable! So why couldn't she accept his explanation?

"When will you be back?" she asked, changing the subject.

James paused. "Next Thursday, I should think. Why? Do you miss me?"

Rachel glanced once more at Mrs. Talbot, but she was obviously engrossed in the film that was in progress. Nevertheless, her voice was stiff as she answered: "Of course."

"Don't sound so enthusiastic about it," he teased. "I gather Mrs. Talbot is with you?"

"Yes." Rachel forced herself to relax. "We're watching television."

"I see." He hesitated. "Have you seen Joel?"

Rachel's relaxation fled, and her fingers tightened round the receiver. *Of course!* she thought furiously. *He was bound to have spoken to his secretary during the last couple of days.*

"Yes. Yes, I've seen him," she replied carefully.

"When?"

Don't you know? Rachel wanted to shout the words at him, but instead she went on quietly: "He came to the Salon to see Miss Grey while we were there."

"Did he?" James sounded annoyed and Rachel wondered whether she had done Miss Clay an injustice. "What did he want?"

Rachel chewed painfully at her lower lip. "I've told you. He came to see Miss Grey."

There was silence for several seconds and then James said: "I hope you're not thinking of telling Joel about Sara's illness."

"Why should I do that?"

"Why indeed? You know of his relationship with Erica Grey now, don't you?"

Rachel licked her lips. "I don't think that's anything to do with me."

"No," he conceded slowly. "Perhaps it's not. I imagine you know well enough the kind of man my son is. What he requires of a woman."

Rachel's nails dug into her palms. "You don't have to illustrate the point, James. I'm not a complete fool!"

"No, my dear, I don't believe you are. Nevertheless, I feel it's my duty to protect you." He paused. "But now, for more important matters. I have decided it would be a good idea if we formally announce our engagement before – before Sara's operation."

"Before?" Rachel was shocked.

"Yes." James sounded thoughtful. "After all, as James Kingdom's fiancée, you will be offered certain privileges, and it seems to me a more suitable arrangement in every way. "We don't want this to be a hole-and-corner affair, Rachel, do we? Certain formalities are expected of me, and I feel that to wait until afterwards would necessitate undue haste and perhaps lack of dignity. I thought a small gathering at somewhere like the Savoy perhaps, a formal announcement after dinner . . . What do you think?"

"I – don't know what to think." That at least was the truth.

"The sooner Joel and Francis accept that I'm going through with this marriage, the better I shall like it. Then, when Sara is well enough to travel, we can have a quiet wedding before leaving for Lyarchos."

Rachel was silent for so long that at last he said: "Rachel?" and she had to find something to say quickly. "If – if that's what you want," she managed slowly.

"Isn't it what you want, too?" he asked sharply, and she hastened to reassure him.

"Of course it is, James. It's just – meeting all your friends and acquaintances! What will they think of me?"

The brief irritation in his tones disappeared. "My dear, they'll all be sick with envy. I can't wait to see the sensation you'll cause. And that reminds me, did you get some clothes from Erica's salon?"

"Clothes!" Rachel steadied her voice. "I had no idea that one woman could own so many clothes!"

He sounded pleased. "And I'm longing to see you wearing them," he exclaimed. "Will you meet me at the airport on my return?"

"If you'd like me to."

"I would." He sighed regretfully. "And now I must go. I'm telephoning from the house of Herr Hartz, one of the delegates to the conference I'm attending, and I'm not sure he'll appreciate this extended addition to his telephone bill." He chuckled. "Give my love to Sara, when you see her tomorrow, and tell her I'm bringing her a very special present from Frankfurt."

Rachel wished she could feel more gratitude as she replaced the receiver. After all, many women would envy her the opportunity to become the wife of one of the wealthiest men in London. Why then did she continually feel like a mouse caught in the claws of a rather sophisticated cat? What he was asking of her was little enough if it meant the difference between life and death to Sara. James was a generous man. She would not want for anything. But there was more to marriage than a standard of living. And she still wasn't absolutely sure that Miss Clay hadn't told him about Joel taking Sara away with him.

Mrs. Talbot departed soon after nine the following morning much to Rachel's relief. She had dreaded the possibility of having to find an excuse for Joel's appearance at the flat, and she determined that when James came home she would make a clean breast of everything that had happened. *Everything?*

Refusing to torture her mind with any more anxieties, she went to the hospital to collect Sara, and wished her smile was as innocent as the child's.

"What are we going to do today, Mummy?" Sara asked, as they walked back to the flat in hazy sunshine. "I think it's going to be a lovely day. Could we go sightseeing again?"

Rachel sighed and looked down at her daughter. "As a matter of fact, Mr. Kingdom is coming to take us out for lunch," she said reluctantly, and felt a pang as Sara's mouth lifted at the corners.

"Joel? Is he? Is he honestly? Ooh, where do you think he will take us? Do you think we might go to the seaside?"

"I shouldn't think so," replied Rachel dampeningly. "It's too cold."

"It's not cold at all!"

"Well, it's too cold for the seaside," retorted Rachel, and then felt mean as Sara's mouth drooped again "Oh, let's wait and see, shall we? Tell me about the hospital. Was everyone kind to you?"

Joel arrived soon after eleven, while Rachel was sharing a mid-morning glass of milk with Sara. She had not expected him to arrive so early, and she had just taken the pins out of her hair and was in the process of brushing it when the door-bell rang. Sara went excitedly to answer it, and Rachel hastily sought to loop her hair into the chignon in which she normally wore it. But her hands were unsteady in her haste, and it was tumbling about her shoulders again in a silky curtain when he came into the room.

This morning Joel was wearing a navy denim suit, with a short battle jacket over a lighter blue collarless sweat shirt, and she thought, albeit unwillingly, how well the casual clothes became his lean body. His eyes flickered coolly over her green pants and scarlet shirt and then narrowed as they came to rest on the unknowingly sensuous beauty of her hair.

"Don't coil it up like that," he said harshly. "Leave it loose!"

But Rachel turned away. "It's much too long to leave loose," she retorted, and continued looping it on to her nape.

"Mummy said you're going to take us out for lunch," put in Sara in a small voice, and after a moment's hesitation Joel turned to the child. He bent and swung her up into his arms smiling into her eyes.

"Yes, I am," he agreed, nodding. "Good heavens, you're a heavy bundle! What do you weigh? Half a ton?"

Sara giggled. "No. I only weigh two stones. I know, because Doctor Lorrimer said so."

"Doctor Lorrimer?" Joel frowned. "Who is Doctor Lorrimer?"

"Joel!" Rachel turned an imploring face in his direction.

"Did I say something wrong?"

"You don't question a child!"

"You do if you don't get answers elsewhere."

"I'll answer your questions."

"Will you?" Joel's lips twisted. "How about – why are you marrying my father, then?"

Sara's mouth puckered. "Oh, why are you two arguing again? You're always arguing! You said you were friends!"

Joel sighed, the tension leaving his features. "We are – friends," he assured her gently. "Now, are you ready?"

Sara had to go to the bathroom and while she was gone, Rachel finished fastening her hair and pulled on the short suede jacket she had brought to wear with her slacks. She was avoiding Joel's eyes, but his voice arrested her:

"I mean to find out, you know. By fair means – or foul "

Rachel looked up at him. "And that's something you know a lot about, don't you? Foul means!"

Joel moved his head slowly from side to side in an attitude of perplexity. "You enjoy saying things like that, don't you? What does it do for you? Does it give you satisfaction to be able to taunt me knowing full well that while Sara's around, you're safe?"

Rachel tried to shrug her shoulders indifferently. "I only say what I feel – what I feel is the truth."

"And to hell with the consequences, is that it?"

"Do you deny that you deserve the things I say to you?" she demanded fiercely.

"Would it make any difference if I did?"

"Not a lot."

"That's what I thought."

"You think you're very clever, don't you?"

"Let's say I don't think *you're* very clever," he retorted smoothly.

"I don't think you're in a position to judge."

"Perhaps not. There are several points about this affair which don't add up. But they will, given time."

"I shouldn't count on that."

"But I do. I count on it very much." His smile was not pleasant. "And you're going to provide the answers for me, aren't you?"

Rachel clenched her fists. "Why don't you ask your father why he's marrying me?"

"Do you think I haven't?"

"And what did he say?" she asked tremulously.

"Why should I tell you? I want to hear your side of the story."

"I don't think he told you anything!" declared Rachel, fumbling with the buttons of her coat. "If he had, you wouldn't be so interested in my motives."

Joel inclined his head. "All right, I'll grant you that point. But it's pretty obvious, even to someone as amoral as me, that *love* doesn't enter into it."

"You don't know that."

"Don't I? Don't I? Then why didn't you tell me that in the beginning?" His lips curled contemptuously. "Oh, Rachel, you don't love my father. His money, perhaps – but not my father."

Her fingers stung across his cheek almost before he had finished speaking, but he made no move to prevent her. He simply smiled, as though her action had merely verified what he had said, and then shifting his gaze to some point beyond her, said: "You're ready, Sara? Good. Let's go."

How Rachel collected her bag and Sara's anorak and followed the others down the stairs to the waiting Mercedes, she could never afterwards remember. She felt too numb, and the day stretched ahead, cold and treacherous. She should never have agreed to come, she told herself despairingly, when Sara was installed in the back and she had to join Joel in the front of the car, but she hadn't been given much choice, had she?

CHAPTER SEVEN

RACHEL sat in the hotel lounge and waited impatiently for Joel and Sara to come back. It was over half an hour since they had set off for the amusement arcade, and she was growing tired of having to avoid the bold stares of the two young men seated across the room at the bar. But when Sara had first suggested playing the pinball machines, Rachel had been only too willing to remain where she was and thus gain a little time to compose herself, but now she was beginning to wonder whether she had been wise. Beyond the windows of the hotel, the promenade was practically deserted, and the mist which had driven everyone indoors curled in spirals around the ornamental trees and shrubs in the hotel garden.

When Sara had asked if they might go to the seaside, Joel had told her that that was where he intended taking them, and amid her squeals of delight he had asked Rachel if she had any objections.

"One place is as good as another," she had retorted jerkily, and thereafter he had made no further attempt to draw her into their conversation. But her absence wasn't noticed. At least, not by Sara. Rachel was amazed at the way she chatted with Joel, laughing and joking with him, and asking him questions that Rachel herself wouldn't have dared to ask. It made Rachel wonder whether there was anything special about a blood relationship. Never having known one herself, except with Sara, she couldn't help but notice how easily Joel adapted his conversation to the child's. As for Sara, Rachel had never known her to be so animated with anyone else, although to be honest, Sara had known few people well outside of Andrew Hanson and Colonel Frenshaw.

They had driven south on the A23, and Rachel had guessed that Joel was taking them to Brighton. It had been a beautiful spring morning in London, and at any other time she would have looked forward to a brisk walk along the promenade after having lunch in one of the hotels. But circumstances being what they were, the prospects were not encouraging, and to add to her depression, Brighton was swathed in a damp sea-fret that made walking on the promenade out of the question.

They had arrived just before one o'clock, and to counter Sara's disappointment, Joel had promised to take her into an amusement arcade after lunch. He had forgone his pre-lunch drink so that they could go straight into the restaurant, and even Rachel had had to admit that the food was excellent. The pity of it was, she could hardly eat a thing.

If Joel noticed her lack of appetite, he made no comment upon it, concentrating on Sara who ate a good meal, and who appreciated his attentions so much more.

They had had coffee in the lounge afterwards, and that was when Sara began agitating about the amusement arcade. As Rachel had not finished her second cup of coffee, it was not too difficult for her to make an excuse not to go with them, and Sara had been quite happy to go off with Joel. Joel himself had perhaps been less keen to leave her on her own, but his polite offer to wait until she was ready had been summarily dismissed by both of his guests, and with an indifferent shrug of his shoulders he had turned away.

But now Rachel was wishing she had not refused his offer. He had made no promise as to how long they might be, and she could not go on sitting in this lounge for ever. Equally, she had no particular desire to go out in the chill damp air and possibly lose her way in the mist.

With a sigh, she got to her feet, draping the strap of her bag over her shoulder. Perhaps if she walked a little way along the promenade she would find the arcade where Joel had taken Sara.

Ignoring the several pairs of eyes which followed her progress across the lounge, she went through the reception area and down the steps of the hotel. Shivering a little in her suede jacket, she drew the collar close about her throat. If anything, the mist seemed thicker than before, and she hesitated doubtfully before setting off.

"I shouldn't worry about him," commented an unexpected voice somewhere near her ear, and she swung round to confront one of the men who had been watching her from the bar.

"I beg your pardon," she said stiffly.

"Your husband! That chap who went off with your little girl. I shouldn't worry about him."

"I think you're making a mistake – "

The man grinned. "No, he made the mistake, love, leaving a dish like you on your own. What happened? Did you have a row?"

"Please go away and leave me alone!" Rachel looked round for assistance, but short of going back into the hotel there was no one she could call on. "My – er – my husband and my daughter are coming back for me."

"Are they? I shouldn't count on it. He looked pretty mad to me when he left here!"

"Go away!"

Rachel's breathing had quickened. Such a thing had never happened to her before, and even now she hardly believed that it could be.

"Come on! Come back inside and have a drink with me and my mate," suggested the man, trying to take her arm. "You won't find anyone in this fog."

"If you don't go away – "

"*Rachel!*"

Joel's angry exclamation had never been more welcome. He

came striding through the garden with Sara at his heels, and she ran to meet him, hardly aware that she ran into his arms. For a moment she pressed herself against him, shuddering, and then he propelled her away from him and demanded: "What is it? What was that man saying to you?"

Rachel gathered herself with difficulty. "Oh – oh, nothing much." She glanced back over her shoulder, but the man had disappeared, back into the hotel no doubt. "It – it was stupid really. I got tired of sitting in the hotel, and you were gone so long!"

"I didn't think you'd miss me!" remarked Joel dryly, and then Sara tugged at her mother's hand and he let her go.

"We met this man who was a friend of Joel's and he owned this boat and he said that if I came back on another day when it wasn't misty he would take me out in it. Can I, Mummy? Can I?"

"Not now, Sara," said Joel, shaking his head. "Your mother's had a – slight shock." He switched his gaze to Rachel. "He went into the hotel. That man who was molesting you – do you want me to go after him?"

Rachel quickly shook her head. "Oh, no. No." She licked her lips. "He wasn't molesting me really. He – he was just – getting fresh, I suppose. Besides, there were two of them in the hotel."

Joel's mouth was wry. "Is that meant to scare me? Or do you care that I might get hurt?"

Rachel moved her shoulders defensively. "A – a little of both, I suppose," she murmured, avoiding his eyes.

Joel hesitated a moment longer, and then he heaved a sigh. "Come on," he said, taking Sara's hand. "Let's find somewhere to have afternoon tea. Then I'll drive you back to town."

The journey back to London was, for Rachel, a much more pleasant experience than the journey to Brighton had been.

Deliberately keeping the conversation on an impersonal level, Joel could be an amusing companion, and Sara was delighted that Rachel was now joining in their chatter.

But Sara was tired, and eventually she fell asleep on the rear seat of the car and then Joel said: "It hasn't been a very successful day, has it?"

"In what way?" Rachel glanced sideways at him.

"I took you both to Brighton because I imagined we would have some time to talk while Sara was climbing about the beach. It didn't work out that way, did it?"

"It didn't begin very well either," murmured Rachel, half to herself, but he heard her.

"For which I'm to blame, I assume," he remarked, without emotion.

"I didn't say that."

"And are you going to talk to me?"

"We're talking now, aren't we?"

"No." His fingers slid smoothly round the wheel as he negotiated a slow-moving wagon. "We're exchanging words, that's all."

"Oh, Joel, why do you persist in making life difficult? Why can't you accept that I'm going to marry your father, and that's all there is to it?"

"I can't accept that."

"You must."

"Rachel, Sara's my daughter. My flesh and blood. And I'm damned if I'm going to give her up without a fight!"

Rachel's fingers curled into her palms. "Joel, you have your career. That's what you always wanted."

"It's what I thought I always wanted!"

She shook her head helplessly. "Are you sure it's not just selfishness that's motivating your concern?"

His fingers tightened on the wheel until the bones showed through the brown skin. "I let you say a lot to me, Rachel. No one else would get away with half the things you do."

Rachel turned her head and stared blindly out of the car window. "I'm not asking for your indulgence."

"No, damn you, I know you're not." Joel swore softly, and then controlled himself again. "Look, I'm trying to be reasonable. Can't you at least meet me half-way?"

"There is no halfway mark with us, Joel, and you know it."

"I know you're not as indifferent to me as you'd have me believe!" he muttered harshly.

Rachel flushed. "I don't think calling one another names will get us anywhere – "

"I am not calling you names. I am merely stating facts. When I kissed you at the flat, you didn't exactly repulse me, did you?"

"What good will bringing that up do?"

"Why not?" He glanced at her. "I should have thought it was a perfectly relevant point to make."

"Just because – just because I was taken aback when you grabbed me, it doesn't mean that I'm secretly harbouring a hopeless passion for you!" she snapped angrily. "Strange as it may seem, I do not find you irresistible!"

There was a pregnant silence and when she ventured to look at him again she felt a ridiculous sense of contrition at the lines of strain that etched his mouth. She had no reason to feel sorry for him. Joel Kingdom was quite capable of taking care of himself. She was a fool to give him a second thought after the way he had treated her. How dared he imagine that because he was the father of the child she had borne that he was entitled to any consideration whatsoever?

They were running through the suburbs now, and the noise of the traffic woke Sara so she sat up on the seat and began chattering again about her proposed boat trip. Although Rachel guessed that Joel was not feeling much like talking right now, he was very patient with the child, and she was grateful for that. Thankfully, Sara noticed nothing amiss in their attitudes to one another.

Joel brought the car to a halt before the entrance to the flats, and Sara frowned when only her mother made to get out. "Aren't you coming in, Joel?" she invited innocently, and Rachel exchanged glances with him hastily.

"I – yes. Yes, come in," she seconded awkwardly, still half concerned about him in spite of herself. "I can give you some tea and a sandwich, if you're interested."

Joel hesitated, his fingers closing round the steering wheel. "And Mrs. Talbot?" he questioned flatly. "Won't she find it odd?"

"Mrs. Talbot's not there," exclaimed Sara, at once. "She left this morning. She only stayed with Mummy last night while I was in hospital!"

Rachel thrust her legs jerkily out of the the car, but Joel was out before her, locking his door and closing hers as she fumbled in her bag for her key.

"So you were in hospital last night, were you, poppet?" he asked, swinging Sara up on to his shoulders without effort. "Mummy didn't tell me about that." And there was a steely hardness to his tones now.

They took the lift up to the flat, and Rachel kept her head bent, dreading the moment when she would have to tell Joel the truth. Because it would have to come out now. If she didn't tell him, he'd find some other way to learn what was wrong with Sara.

But to her relief, when they entered the flat, he said no more about it right then, making himself at home on the couch, admiring the toys that Sara brought for his inspection, and eventually submitting to her pleas to be "drawn" again. He sketched a full-length portrait of her as she played with Helga and her other dolls, and because it was in her sketchbook, she told Rachel it was her very own picture.

Rachel busied herself in the kitchen. She had bought some bread on her way home from the hospital that morning, and there were plenty of eggs to make omelettes instead of the sandwiches she had initially thought of. She opened a large tin of chicken soup and poured it into a saucepan to warm, and whipped some cream to add to a tinned fruit salad that she served in dessert dishes.

The meal was a success. Hunger had sharpened her own appetite, and she refused to think too far ahead. Joel sat at the opposite end of the kitchen table, having shed his denim jacket, his arms protruding from the short sleeves of the sweat shirt, tanned and muscular. If ever she caught his eyes upon her, their coldness warned her that he was not finished with her yet, but mostly he talked to Sara, and she was the link between them.

"That was delicious," he said at last, finishing his second cup of tea, but looking at Sara. "How about you and me doing the washing up for Mummy?"

"All right." This was something new for Sara, never having been part of a family. "But can I wash?"

Rachel sat uneasily in the living room while Joel and Sara dealt with the dishes. She could hear Sara splashing in the water, and giggling at the things Joel was saying to her, and wondered why it couldn't have been James she responded to in that way. But then James had never played with her. He had talked to her, of course, made a fuss of her – bought her things, even. But there was not the rapport between them that there apparently was between her and – and her *father* . . .

Rachel got to her feet and paced impatiently about the room. She was becoming maudlin. This could well be a passing fancy for Joel, a diversion before something else diverted his attention. Wasn't that all *she* had been to him?

When they came into the living room a few minutes later, Sara was looking rather anxious. "My jersey's all wet,

Mummy," she said, plucking at it worriedly. "I'm sorry."

"It was my fault," put in Joel abruptly. "It will dry, won't it?"

His eyes challenged her, but Rachel couldn't withstand his compelling stare. "I – yes. It's all right, Sara," she assured the little girl hastily. "Besides, it's bedtime. You can go and take off all your clothes now and I'll put you in the bath."

"Could Joel put me in the bath?" exclaimed Sara, at once, and Rachel sighed rather irritably.

"No. No, Sara, I'll do that – "

"If Sara – " began Joel, but Rachel silenced him with an angry look.

"I'll bathe you, Sara," she asserted firmly. "Go along now."

"What's the matter, Rachel?" Joel demanded, as Sara went reluctantly out of the room. "Are you afraid I'll see the fistula?" His lips twisted as her eyes widened in dismay. "That is what's wrong with her, isn't it? Kidney disease?"

All through Sara's bath and afterwards, putting on her pyjamas, brushing her hair, Rachel thought about what Joel had said, and realised there was no point in pretending any longer. Sooner or later he would have to know anyway, she thought wearily.

Sara wanted a glass of milk for her supper, and then she went to say goodnight to Joel, who was waiting in the living room.

"Will you come and tuck me in?" she asked, small and appealing in her sprigged cotton pyjamas.

Rachel, watching Joel's face, saw the stirring emotion that tautened his jawline, and wondered if he would have felt differently about children had he found a woman he really wanted to marry. Perhaps the reason he was behaving differently now was because he *had* found that woman. Certainly Erica Grey played no small role in his life. It crossed Rachel's mind with a terrifying pang that had Joel learned of Sara's existence in other circumstances, he might well have wanted to adopt her – he and Erica. He would have had quite a case, she had to concede. And with the kind of lawyers he could afford to retain ...

Her voice was therefore brusque, as she explained: "Oh, do hurry up, Sara. It's after seven."

"I want Joel to come!" Sara repeated, with annoying insistence.

Joel got to his feet. "Why not?" He looked down at Sara with an indulgent smile. "Come on – show me where you sleep."

Rachel accompanied them into the bedroom, but after kissing Sara goodnight she left them and went back into the living room. As she did so, the phone rang, and her nerves jangled with the sound. She could guess who it would be, but she had to answer it.

"Hello?" she said quietly.

"Rachel? Rachel, is that you?"

James's voice was just as compelling, and Rachel drew an unsteady breath before replying: "Yes. Yes, James, it's me."

"Are you all right? You sound – nervous."

"No, I'm not. Not really." Rachel forced her voice to remain steady with great difficulty. "Actually, I – I was putting Sara to bed."

"How is she? Did all go well last night?"

"Yes. Yes, everything went fine. How are you, James?"

"As usual, in the peak of condition." He chuckled. "How about you? Are you having an exciting time in London?"

"Hardly an exciting time, James."

"Why not? Miss Clay told you I'd opened an account for you at Harrods, didn't she? I've been imagining you enjoying a spending spree."

Rachel sighed. "No. No, Miss Clay must have forgotten to

tell me that. But don't – don't trouble her, James, really. I – I'm not the type to spend money that freely."

"Nonsense! All women like spending money. I shall speak to Miss Clay first thing in the morning."

Rachel wanted to protest, but she knew from past experience that it would do no good. Once James made up his mind about something he was a very determined man. Her hand holding the receiver to her ear trembled slightly. His son was more like him than he cared to admit.

"In any case," James went on, "I thought I should keep you in the picture so far as the arrangements for our engagement party are concerned. Certain preliminary arrangements have already been made, and I wondered if there was anyone you particularly wanted to ask."

Rachel shook her head, and then realising he couldn't see her, said: "I don't think so." The only people she could have asked were now living on the Continent, and she did not think either Colonel Frenshaw or his secretary would make the journey to London for such an event.

"Very well, then." James didn't sound disappointed, on the contrary, he sounded relieved, and Rachel guessed that he would not have welcomed any of her contemporaries from the orphanage with any degree of enthusiasm. No doubt, like the sons he had fathered, he hoped to mould her to some idealistic image of his own making.

Rachel sensed, rather than heard, Joel come into the room behind her. He didn't say anything, but she was conscious of his brooding presence. It made her nervous, and she said rather abruptly: "Is that all, then?"

There was silence for a long moment, and at last James responded: "Are you sure there's nothing troubling you, Rachel? You seem a little – distraught."

Rachel caught her breath. "I've told you, James, I'm fine, really. I – I have a headache, that's all."

Joel made a disbelieving sound behind her, and moved into the room, lighting a cheroot. But fortunately, James was offering his sympathy and heard nothing untoward.

"Why didn't you say so?" he asked now. "I expect it's the change of air. Langthwaite may have been remote, but it was far from the fumes of diesel oil." He paused. "Very well, my dear, I'll ring off. Oh, and by the way, I'm hoping to be back on Tuesday instead of Thursday. I'll let you know the time of arrival of my flight later. Give my love to Sara, won't you?"

"I will. Goodbye, James."

"*Auf weidersehen, liebling*. You see, I'm learning the language."

Rachel made some suitable reply and then replaced her receiver, turning reluctantly to face Joel who was standing before the hearth.

"*Liebling*," he commented, with cold mockery, revealing he had heard all of their conversation since he entered the room. "My father is getting sentimental in his old age."

"Must you be so unpleasant?" Rachel went to the windows and drew the curtains against the darkness outside. "I suppose you think discovering Sara's weakness entitles you to be so objectionable."

Joel exhaled heavily. "I think I was entitled to know the truth about her condition," he replied forcefully. "A 'minor blood deficiency' was a totally misleading understatement of fact. Sara needs a dialyser, doesn't she? That's why she stayed in hospital last night."

"All right, all right!" Rachel turned back to him, folding her hands tightly together. "I'll tell you the truth. You'll have to know sooner or later ..." She looked down at her linked fingers. "Sara was born with a congenital malformation of her kidneys."

"Go on." Joel's face was grim.

"Well – " Rachel sought for words, "we – I didn't know at

first. She seemed a normal, healthy baby. She was never big for her age, and she didn't gain weight very quickly, but nor did a lot of other babies." She sighed. "From being very small, she was – prone to infection. The mildest kind of virus seemed to cause her to run high temperatures and suffer gastric disturbances, and – eventually we discovered what was wrong."

"And?"

"Oh, Joel, give me time." Rachel sank down weakly into an armchair, staring blindly into the glowing coals of the electric fire burning in the grate. She moved her shoulders. "She saw doctors, specialists. They did everything they could, but it was never enough. Six months ago she suffered renal failure. That was when the dialysis began."

"God!" Joel paced restlessly about the room. "And even then you never thought to tell me!"

"Why should I?" Rachel looked up at him defensively. "It wasn't your worry, it was mine. I had chosen to bring Sara into the world. I was responsible for her."

"But in the circumstances – "

"The circumstances had nothing to do with anything. They were an unfortunate accident of nature. Retribution perhaps, for the way I had behaved!"

"Oh, God, don't talk such rubbish!" he muttered savagely. "What did you do, for heaven's sake? Except walk out on me!"

"Well, these things have been known to be hereditary, and it's possible that my parents, whoever they were – "

"Sara has two parents, too."

"But there's been nothing like that in your family, has there?" she exclaimed tremulously.

"Hasn't there?" Joel's brows had drawn together.

"Oh, Joel, don't bait me, please." She got to her feet again, and walked round the back of the couch. "Well, anyway, that was the situation six months ago, and – "

"Where does my father come into all this?" he interrupted her.

"He – that is – Colonel Frenshaw was having to sell up and go and live abroad. For health reasons, you see. Your father's bank handled all his investments."

"And – my father came to see the Colonel, I suppose."

"Yes. They'd known one another years ago, in London."

"How coincidental!"

"Do you think I planned it that way?" she demanded hotly. "I nearly died of shock when I opened the door and found James Kingdom on the step. Naturally, he asked the Colonel about me, and when he saw Sara ..."

"Yes. With his foreknowledge, he guessed what you had done." Joel's fists clenched. "But that still doesn't explain why you're marrying him. Has he promised you financial help for Sara? Is there some obscure surgeon somewhere who has perfected a cure for which you have to pay?"

"No. No, at least – it's a simple enough solution really. Your father's blood cell groupings match Sara's. He's agreed to a transplant of one of his own kidneys."

CHAPTER EIGHT

"*What?*" Joel stared at her in horror. "But my father's an old man!"

"Not so old." Rachel's fingers nervously massaged the back of the couch. "Besides, his kidneys are healthy, and apparently perfectly suitable for transplant."

"You can't be serious!" Joel wiped the back of his hand across his forehead. "My God, and you're marrying him for that!"

"Among other things." Rachel dug her nails into the cloth. "Joel, it hasn't been easy, caring for a child like Sara. At least, with James, she'll have every advantage."

Joel crushed out his cheroot with unsteady fingers. "I could give her the same advantages!" he muttered.

Rachel's breathing was shallow. "Financially, perhaps," she conceded.

He looked up, his eyes cold. "What else is there?"

Rachel looked away from him. "I wouldn't expect you to understand."

"That's good. Because I don't." Joel flexed his shoulder muscles impatiently. "I won't let you do it."

"You can't stop me."

"Can't I?" He unfastened the two top buttons of his sweat shirt and massaged his throat. "I wouldn't bank on that if I were you."

"Oh, Joel!" Rachel felt near to tears now. "Joel, can't we stop this continual bickering? You don't really care about Sara – or me. You have your work – and Erica Grey – "

"Let's keep Erica out of this, shall we?"

"Why should I? You can't deny the relationship you have with her."

"I don't intend to. Erica and I are two adult people. I admit that from time to time – "

"I don't want to know!"

Rachel turned away and put her hands over her ears, and she was not aware he had come round the couch to stand behind her until she felt the warmth of his breath fanning her skin. Then she lowered her hands to wrap her arms defensively around her.

"Oh, Rachel!" He spoke huskily, sliding one hand under the coil of her hair and stroking the sensitive nape of her neck. "You don't want to know because of what was between us. Don't try to deny it. You should never have gone away and left me. I went through purgatory trying to find you. If I'd known you were pregnant as well . . ." He slid his hand over one of hers, finding her palm with his thumb. "You remember how it always was with us. I admit I behaved selfishly, but try to see it my way. I wanted you – my God! how I wanted you! And you were beautiful, do you know that? I've never made love to any other woman. Sex perhaps – but not love!"

There was a liquid sweetness throbbing through her veins that quickened her pulse and weakened her lower limbs. She knew an aching desire to yield against him and feel the demanding hardness of his body. But she was not fool enough to imagine that the emotions he was deliberately arousing in her were anything more than an instinctive response to his undoubted sensual attraction.

Dragging herself away from him, she turned to face him, hands clenched by her sides, stiffening her resolve with anger. "Don't try to seduce me with words, Joel! I know you too well."

He shrugged, narrowing his eyes, feet apart, making her intensely aware of his dark masculinity. "You can't go through with this, Rachel," he stated in a low voice. "You know you can't."

"I shall go through with it!" she declared fiercely. "And no amount of sexual persuasion on your part is going to stop me!"

Joel stared at her unblinkingly. "I'm prepared to give Sara one of my kidneys. If my father is a suitable donor, I see no reason why I shouldn't be as well."

"*No!*" The word was torn from her. "I want nothing from you!"

"Not even your daughter's health?" he demanded, less coolly now.

"Sara is going to be all right – "

"And if the transplant fails? What then?"

Rachel caught her lip between her teeth. "Why should it fail?"

"What do the doctors say? What are her chances?"

Rachel moved her head helplessly. "They're – reasonable." She drew a trembling breath. "I can't tell you any more than that. I don't understand altogether what's involved."

"So you're sacrificing yourself for the child!" His lips twisted scornfully. "What kind of recompense are you making? What if the operation doesn't succeed? Will it all have been for nothing?"

Rachel held up her head. "James – James and I are not getting married until – until after the operation is over."

"Oh, really?" Joel sneered. "So you imagine if it all goes wrong, my father will call off the deal?"

Rachel's brows drew together. "Why, of course."

Joel gave her a disgusted look. "You can't be serious!"

"What do you mean?"

Joel shook his head. "Well, I understand from Miss Clay that my father is organising a plush engagement party, is that right?"

"I – I believe so."

"To introduce you to his friends and colleagues in the City."

"Y-yes."

Joel drew a deep breath. "And you imagine after all the publicity that will ensue that my father will call the deal off if things don't go well?"

"Why shouldn't he?"

"Oh, Rachel, you can't be for real!" Joel sank down on to the arm of the couch, raking a hand through his hair. "Rachel, men like my father care a lot about their public image. Introducing you as his fiancée will be quite an achievement for a man of his age." He scowled up at her. "Quite an achievement indeed." He paused. Then: "If you try to call the engagement off because Sara isn't going to get well, he'll make mincemeat out of you in the press! Oh, no, Rachel, if you get engaged to my father, you can say goodbye to your freedom!"

"I don't believe you!" Rachel stared at him, her mouth working tremulously. "You're just saying these things to frighten me!"

"Am I?" He raised dark eyebrows. "I shouldn't be too sure of that, if I were you."

"Oh, what's it to you?" she exclaimed unsteadily. "Why should you care, one way or the other?"

"You know the answer to that," he told her, his voice thickening as he reached towards her and grasping her wrist pulled her close to him. "I care what happens to you, Rachel," he muttered. "I never stopped wanting you. I want you now – here."

His eyes were dark with emotion and Rachel's hands pressed desperately against his shoulders. But his shirt didn't come up round his neck, and her fingers encountered his smooth skin. She remembered the feel of his skin so well, and for an instant she thought of James's skin, and of how much more gnarled and lined it was. Joel took one of her hands and pushed it down inside his shirt, cupping her nape with his free hand and forcing her mouth down to his.

She was close against him, but she wanted to be closer. The warmth of his body was a potent intoxicant, and the scent of his skin mingled with the other scents of shaving lotion and tobacco. Her legs were giving out under her, and the effort of pushing herself away from him was almost too much for her. But she made it, and stood, breathing heavily, her hair loose and silky about her flushed face.

"I hate you, Joel Kingdom!" she stormed furiously, dragging her unbuttoned shirt across her pointed breasts. "Get out of here! I wish I never had to see you again!"

Joel, who since her abrupt withdrawal had been sitting with his hands hanging loosely between his legs, got slowly to his feet, and thrust his shirt back into his pants. There was a faintly glazed look about his eyes, but his mouth hardened when he encountered Rachel's indignant glare.

"I'm sorry I can't oblige you on the second count," he commented ironically, picking up his jacket and pulling it on. "As for the first – you're fooling yourself, Rachel. You don't hate me." His mouth curled contemptuously. "But, God forgive me, if you go through with this, I'll hate you!"

Rachel lay awake long into the night. Her body ached and she refused to admit the reasons why. Some wanton part of her yearned for Joel and the satisfaction of the senses he could give her, and she desperately tried to escape the torture of these forbidden thoughts. She had never permitted herself to think of that night they had spent together, always cloaking it in its subsequent veil of treachery and humiliation, but tonight, after those disturbing minutes in Joel's arms, the memories would not be denied. If only he had wanted to marry her ... But happiness like that was a mirage with a man like Joel Kingdom. She understood that he wanted her, that she could arouse him without too much difficulty; but a relationship built on the shifting sands of physical attraction was not what she wanted. She had loved Joel – loved him with all the wealth of tenderness and passion of which she was capable. And he had taken her love, and destroyed it ...

The next morning Rachel told Sara that she was taking her shopping. She did want to buy the little girl some new clothes, but her primary motives were to escape from the flat before Joel had time to appear.

"Won't we be seeing Joel today?" Sara asked, rather disappointedly, as they walked down to the bus stop, and Rachel felt an impatient sense of frustration.

"No," she replied firmly. "Mr. – er – Joel has his work to attend to. He hasn't the time to spend with us."

"But last night he said he would come and take me to the Zoo today," complained Sara sulkily. "How do you know he won't come while we're out?"

"I don't know that," retorted Rachel, and then tried to reason with her. "I expect Uncle James will take you to the Zoo, if you ask him to."

"I don't want to go with Uncle James!" replied Sara, and even refused to go upstairs on the bus as was her usual habit.

The shopping expedition was not a success. Sara had to be coerced into trying clothes on, and even then her pale features and turned down mouth made pretty dresses and pants suits look less than attractive. For once, the fact that she was small for her age was an advantage. Assistants took her for a three- or four-year-old, and excused her on those grounds. But Rachel refused to be put off and when they eventually returned home after having lunch in town, Sara was the indifferent possessor of three dresses, two pants suits, some underwear, a new anorak and a rather extravagant suede coat for special occasions.

There was no sign of Joel, much to Rachel's relief, and Sara seemed resigned to the fact that for today at least she was not to see him. However, as Rachel got her ready for bed, she said:

"I've decided I'd like Joel to live with us after you and that man get married."

Rachel was taken aback. "Don't be silly, Sara."

"Why is it silly? You'll be his mummy too, won't you? Why shouldn't he live with us?"

"I explained all that before, Sara," retorted Rachel shortly. "Joel Kingdom has – has a home of his own. Besides, we'll be living in Greece."

"Where's Greece?"

"Sara, I told you. It's a long, long way away, where the sun shines all the time."

"I don't want the sun to shine all the time."

"Well, I'm afraid I can't do anything about that."

"You could stay in England. I'd like to stay in England."

"Mr. King – that is, Uncle James – wants to live in Greece. He has an island – I told you. The water's lovely and warm, and you can go swimming."

"I can't swim."

"You'll learn."

"I don't want to learn."

"Sara, I warn you – "

"Well! Why have we to go and live in stuffy old Greece? Why can't you marry Joel instead and live in London?" Her eyes brightened. "Ooh, that would be super, wouldn't it? He'd be my daddy then, wouldn't he?"

"Sara!"

Rachel almost screamed the word, and Sara stared at her curiously. "What's the matter? Why are you looking like that? Just because you're always arguing with him doesn't mean you can't be friends. Joel said that."

"Sara, *please.*" Rachel tucked her into her bed and straightened, her nerves stretched to a fine pitch. "I don't want to hear any more about Joel Kingdom, do you understand? I am going to marry Uncle James, and we're going to live in Greece, and that's the end of the matter. Do I make myself clear?"

Sara looked sulky, but she nodded reluctantly. "Yes, Mummy."

"Good. Now – goodnight."

In the living room, Rachel did something she had never done before. She poured herself a stiff measure of whisky and carrying it to a chair, sat down and began to drink it. The strong spirit caught her throat and caused her to cough, but she persisted until it was all gone and then she poured herself another.

After three whiskys, she was violently sick, and her futile attempt at getting drunk was just an undignified fiasco. However, the painful retching had exhausted her, and to her relief she remembered little after her head touched the pillow that night.

The next day, Rachel awoke with a splitting headache which she assumed was a hangover from her attempted drinking of the night before. She didn't feel at all like getting up and making breakfast, and Sara's downcast little face didn't help. Clearly the child had not forgotten their exchange of words the previous evening, and although she didn't actually mention Joel's name, every time there was some sound outside the flats she rushed to the window to see what it was. In fact after a time Rachel found herself listening for the doorbell or the telephone and she was rather surprised when Joel did not contact them. She had not expected him to give up so easily, and while she told herself that she was glad, he had promised to see Sara again, and she was so easily upset. It wasn't a very pleasant day outside either, so they stayed in the flat, and Sara finally went to bed in a rather tearful mood.

When there was no word from Joel by the afternoon of the following day, Rachel began to feel concerned. Sara lay around the flat, too listless even to play with Helga, refusing even to accompany Rachel when she ran down to the store on the corner for some bread. The television was on, but she paid little attention to it, her cheeks paler and more waxen than ever. In a little over twenty-four hours she was due to go into hospital again for her treatment, but Rachel was very much afraid she would not want to go. She had never known her so depressed, and her resentment turned against Joel. He could have contacted the child, she thought bitterly. And yet what good would it do for Sara to depend on him for anything?

After tea that evening, Rachel suggested a walk. Regent's Park was not too far away, and the fresh air might put a little colour into Sara's cheeks.

But Sara refused to go. "You go," she said indifferently. "I don't feel like walking."

"But, Sara, you haven't been out for two days!"

Sara looked up at her through stormy dark eyes. "And Joel hasn't been here for three days!" she declared, her lips trembling. "What did you say to him? Why did you send him away?"

Rachel pressed her palms together. "I – I didn't send him away," she protested. But was that entirely true? Hadn't she indeed told him that she wished she never had to see him again? "I expect he's busy, Sara. I – he'll come back."

"Will he?" Sara didn't sound convinced. "Well, I'll stay in. He might telephone, mightn't he?"

Rachel sighed. "Sara, this is silly. Joel Kingdom is nothing to do with us."

"I liked him. He liked me. I know he did."

"I'm sure he did, darling, but that doesn't mean . . ." Rachel cast about in her mind for something to say. "Sara, you've got to think about the future. In a few weeks, we'll be going abroad, and then – "

"I've told you, I don't want to go abroad."

Rachel refused to answer this, pacing impatiently about the room. Sara propped herself up on one elbow on the couch and looked at her mother.

"You could ring him," she said, as if the idea had just occurred to her. "Couldn't you, Mummy? Oh, will you, Mummy, will you?"

"No." Rachel regretted the way Sara's fleeting brightness was instantly extinguished. "Sara darling, I can't."

"Why can't you? Don't you know the number?"

That would have been a simple lie, but Rachel couldn't tell it. Besides, Sara was too intelligent. She would know that there were ways of finding it out.

"Sara, he might have people at the flat. Visitors. He may be working ..."

"Heron could answer the phone."

Rachel shook her head. Sara had all the answers.

"And what do you expect me to say to him?" she exclaimed, frustratedly.

"Tell him – tell him I want to see him. I do, Mummy, I do!"

Rachel walked restlessly across the carpet. Ring Joel and tell him that Sara wanted to see him? It was ludicrous! Particularly after the way they had parted ...

"I can't do that, Sara."

Sara's eyes filled with tears. "You mean you won't, *you won't*!" Two hectic splashes of colour appeared on her cheeks, and Rachel knew she was working herself up into hysteria.

"Sara, be reasonable – "

"Go away. Go away, and leave me alone! I don't want to see you. I want to see Joel, I want to see Joel!"

Rachel's hands balled into fists as she stared at her daughter's shuddering body, and something seemed to snap inside her.

"Oh, all right, *all right*," she exclaimed tautly, and crossing the floor picked up the receiver and dialled the number before indecision could prevent her. In all these years, she had never forgotten Joel's number, and that knowledge would have troubled her if she had given it a second thought.

The bell seemed to ring for ages before the receiver was lifted at the other end. Rachel had already decided that Joel was out, and when Heron gave their number and enquired who was speaking she was tempted to slam the receiver down again.

But Sara's tear-stained face forced her to identify herself and ask to speak to Mr. Kingdom.

"I'm afraid Mr. Kingdom is resting and cannot be disturbed, Mrs. Gilmour," Heron stated politely and apologetically. "Can I give him a message?"

Rachel ground her teeth together. Resting – and not to be disturbed! She felt sickened by the knowledge. Who was there with him that he had not to be disturbed?

"No," she said, watching Sara's face all the time she was speaking. "No, there's no message."

When she replaced the receiver, Sara sat up. "What is it?" she demanded. "Where is he? Why didn't you speak to him?"

Rachel forced herself to speak casually: "He – he's in bed. I don't think – he's very well."

She was hardly prepared for Sara's reactions to this "Why? What's the matter with him? Is he ill? Can we go and see him?"

"No, Sara."

"Why not?"

"Because we can't." Rachel spread her hands. "Look, Heron will tell him I rang when he gets up. If he wants to contact us, he will."

"I don't believe you." Sara was tearful again. "You're just saying that!"

"I'm not." Rachel didn't know how to convince her. She supposed in another child – a healthy child – Sara's behaviour could be construed as the result of too much spoiling, but the truth was it wasn't like her to behave so disobediently, to throw tantrums over nothing. She genuinely cared what happened to Joel. What a pity that concern was so misplaced.

"Why don't you like Joel?" the child was asking now. "Why don't you want to go and see him?"

"Sara, we can't do anything until he – until he's better."

"Why not?"

"Because we can't."

"When will he be better?"

"How should I know?"

Sara slid off the couch and came over to her. "Please, Mummy, couldn't we just go to his apartment and see him? I'd be ever so good. I wouldn't make any noise or anything. We could just say we were worried about him. We could take him some flowers."

Rachel bit back the retort she was tempted to make. "Where would we get flowers at this time of the evening?"

"Well, some sweeties, then."

Rachel was nearing the end of her tether. It was all so simple in Sara's eyes. Joel's manservant had said he was resting, therefore he must be ill! Rachel glanced irritably at her watch. Half past six! She couldn't – she *wouldn't* believe that that was the truth.

She saw Sara's appealing little face staring up at her and suddenly came to a decision. Perhaps she should take the child to Joel's apartment. Heron was there. He would have his orders. If Sara heard it from him, she might begin to believe that Joel was not the god she imagined him to be.

"All right," she said reluctantly. "We'll go to the flat. But if Heron refuses to let you see Joel, you have to accept it, do you understand?"

Sara's lips quivered. "He won't do that, will he?"

"I don't know. I can't tell you. You'll have to wait and see."

Rachel spoke deliberately offhandedly. Better that she should be prepared for the cracks in his armour.

They took a taxi to Breton Towers, that luxurious apartment building overlooking Regent's Park where Joel occupied the penthouse. It was a painful experience for Rachel returning there. She recalled her last interview in Joel's apartment with acute distress and humiliation.

They took the lift to the penthouse floor and Sara reached up to ring Joel's doorbell. The chime-like sound echoed through the apartment, and Rachel's muscles stiffened in nervous anticipation.

But nothing happened. No one came to answer the door, and no sound ensued from within the apartment. Rachel looked down at Sara's troubled face and determinedly rang the bell again. Heron had taken long enough to answer the phone. Perhaps he had been given orders not to open the door to anyone. Well, that was just too bad!

After the third attempt, Sara's face began to crumple. "He's not in, is he?" she asked tearfully. "He isn't really poorly at all. Heron was just saying that, wasn't he?"

Rachel didn't know how to answer her. The disillusionment was evident, it was what she had wanted, but now she wanted to spare her the inevitable distress.

"It's possible that Heron has had to go out," she murmured awkwardly. "Mr. King – that is – Joel might be asleep. Have you thought of that?"

Sara sniffed. "He would have heard the doorbell, wouldn't he?".

"Yes. But he might not come to answer it. He couldn't know it was you, could he?"

The sound of the door behind them being opened brought them both round with a start, and Rachel's instinctive exclamation was drowned by Sara's excited: "*Joel!* Oh, Joel, you are in! Mummy thought you might be!"

Joel leaned heavily against the door, supporting himself with obvious effort. Two days' growth of beard darkened his jawline, and the lines around his eyes gave him a haggard look. He was wearing only a hastily pulled on towelling bath-robe, and beads of perspiration dampened his forehead. His hair was tousled and it was obvious that he was not at all well.

"I'm sorry," he muttered, raking his hair back from his forehead. "I wasn't expecting visitors, and Heron's gone out."

Rachel gathered her composure. "We're sorry, too, Joel," she exclaimed, encompassing Sara in her apology. "I – Sara wanted to see you. She was – worried about you."

Joel stepped back against the wall behind him, swaying slightly. "Won't you come in?"

Rachel caught her lower lip between her teeth. "Perhaps we'd better not," she demurred, ignoring Sara's gasp of dismay.

"Please – come in!" Joel winced as a spasm of pain crossed his face. "I – I'll be all right. I've got an almighty headache, that's all."

Rachel looked at him uncertainly. His narrowed eyes betrayed little, concealed as they were by his thick lashes but he was trembling and she knew he wasn't pretending about the headache. It was migraine, of course. She should have guessed. *Oh, ye of little faith*, she thought, with a grimace of self-derision.

Taking Sara's hand, she walked into the flat, stepping down the shallow steps into the main living area. It was like stepping back in time except that the thick milky beige carpet was new and toned well with a long curved velvet couch and armchairs in a rich deep red. Beyond the massive plate glass windows, the roofs and spires of London could be seen through the slats in the long blinds.

Joel closed the door, leaning back against it as he fastened the belt of his bathrobe, and Rachel noticed that his feet were bare.

Meanwhile, Sara had loosened her hand from Rachel's and was meandering round this new domain, picking up objects here and there, probing into cupboards and shelves, touching a pile of drawing materials strewn on a table beneath the windows.

"Sara!"

Rachel's tone was sharply reproving, but Joel made a dismissing gesture. "She's all right," he assured her, rubbing an exploratory hand over the stubble on his chin. "If you'll just give me a few minutes, I'll make myself more presentable."

"No! That is – " Rachel halted awkwardly. "We don't want to disturb you. I – Heron told us that you were – resting, and – "

"Heron?"

Joel looked confused, and Rachel hastened on: "We phoned, about half an hour ago. Maybe a little more." She glanced at her watch. "That was how we knew ..." Her voice trailed away. "We shouldn't have come."

Joel stared at her for a few disturbing moments, and then comprehension seemed to dawn in his eyes. "You thought – oh, yes, I can guess what you thought," he muttered coldly.

Rachel bent her head, and Sara chose that moment to turn and say: "Why haven't you been to see us? You said you would," she reproached him.

Joel transferred his attention to Sara, and moving rather unsteadily away from the door, came down the steps into the main body of the room. "I intended to," he told her gently, going down on his haunches beside her. "But I've felt pretty lousy these past couple of days. Have you missed me?"

Sara put her hands on his shoulders. "Yes, I missed you," she answered gravely. "I waited and waited for you to come and when you didn't I felt poorly, too."

"Did you?" Joel's eyes darkened, and he gathered her close to him for a moment. It was the first time he had held the child like that, and Rachel couldn't bear to watch them. She turned away and walked to the window, and after a minute Joel got to his feet. "I'll go and get dressed."

Rachel turned then. "There's no need. We can go now Sara has seen that you're all right. You'd be better off in bed."

Joel regarded her without emotion. "I am capable of putting some clothes on," he assured her flatly. "I can stand it if you can."

Rachel pressed her palms to her cheeks. "Oh, Joel," she murmured half-heartedly, "I'm sorry I misjudged you. And I am sorry about disturbing you. You don't have to entertain us. I can imagine how you must be feeling."

"I doubt it," he returned enigmatically, and then turned away. "I shan't be long."

While he was gone, Rachel wandered round the room in much the same way as Sara had done, renewing her acquaintance with its lines and angles. She had always liked this room, its height and spaciousness, its elegance and good taste; and yet its atmosphere had a warmth and quality of comfortableness that made one instinctively relax. Someone had arranged a huge bowl of irises and tulips on top of the cowl of the pseudo-log fire, and their colouring was reflected in the warm panelling of the walls. Their perfume was a delicate thing that drifted elusively on the air.

When Joel returned, he was clean-shaven, his hair had been brushed, and he looked lean and sinuously attractive in dark brown leather pants and a cream shirt made of heavy silk. Only the pallor of his cheeks and the dark rings around his eyes revealed that he was by no means recovered.

"Now," he said, swaying in the doorway, "can I get you a drink?"

Rachel took one look at his drawn features and then went

towards him, taking his arm and drawing him towards the couch. "Come and sit down," she said firmly. "I'll get the drinks. What do you want?"

Joel sank down obediently on to the couch, and rested his dark head back against the burgundy velvet upholstery. "Just something long and cool for me, please," he answered, his eyes half closed. "Nothing alcoholic."

There was no ice in the container and leaving Joel and Sara, Rachel went through to the kitchen to get some from the freezer. Her fingers trailed across the light Swedish panelling of the wall units, stroked the steel drainer beside the sink. She remembered preparing occasional suppers for herself and Joel in here when Heron was out, making Joel dry the dishes for her afterwards and always ending up in his arms ...

She poured a glass of lemonade for Sara, iced lime and lemon for Joel, and a dry Martini and soda for herself. Joel drank half of his thirstily, and then said: "I was ready for that."

"Have you had anything to eat today?" Rachel asked anxiously.

"No." Joel shook his head, shuddering in distaste. "I couldn't face food. Not right now."

Sara finished her lemonade and clambered on to his knee, ignoring Rachel's protest. "Are you coming to see us tomorrow?"

Joel tickled her small middle. "We'll see," he promised.

"But you should eat something," Rachel insisted, sitting down on the couch, too, albeit some distance away from him. "Can't I get you anything?"

Joel looked at her out of the corners of his eyes. "You could tell me you're not going to marry my father," he said quietly. "That would be powerful medicine."

"I can't do that." Rachel's hands tightened round her glass.

"Let me do what I can for you," he muttered. "Give me the chance!"

"No!"

Rachel got to her feet again, and as she did so the doorbell chimed. She turned questioning eyes on Joel, and an expression of resignation crossed his face. "Don't answer it," he said as she would have mounted the steps. "I don't want to see anyone else."

But Sara, with her usual enthusiasm for opening doors, wasn't listening to him. As he was speaking she had slid off his knee, and before either of them could stop her, she was reaching up to open the door.

Erica Grey stared at the child in amazement as she came into the apartment, and then her small features hardened when she saw Rachel. "Am I interrupting anything?" she enquired, with obvious indifference to the answer. Then she saw Joel who was getting unsteadily to his feet. "Oh, Joel darling, you're not well! Why didn't you let me know? I've been trying to get hold of you, and all I get out of Heron is that you're not to be disturbed!"

Sara had closed the door behind the visitor and was standing staring with unconcealed dislike at the woman who was clinging to Joel's arm. Then she looked at her mother, and Rachel saw the way her lower lip was trembling.

"I think we ought to be going, Sara," she asserted quietly. "It's getting late. Past your bedtime."

"No – wait!" Joel disentangled himself from Erica and took a step foward. "Rachel, don't go yet."

"If I'm intruding ..." Heavy sarcasm tinged Erica's voice, and Rachel felt terrible.

"No, you're not. Sara – "

"We haven't finished talking yet, Rachel." Joel cast an impatient glance in Erica's direction. "Please stay."

Sara pursed her lips. "I want to go to the bathroom," she announced tremulously, and Erica made a sound of disgust.

"You know where it is, don't you?" Joel looked across at

the little girl. "I showed you the other day, do you remember?"

Sara nodded, and ignoring all of them marched out of the room. After she had gone, Rachel twisted the strap of her handbag round her wrist and moved towards the door, ready for departure.

"Rachel!" Joel grimaced as the effort of speaking pounded through his head. He grasped the back of the couch to support himself and took another couple of steps. "Rachel, for God's sake!"

Erica stared at him in astonishment. "Joel, what is going on here?"

Joel turned tormented eyes in her direction. Then he nodded. "Yes," he said heavily, as though coming to a decision. "Yes, it's time you were told."

"*Joel –* "

Rachel tried to silence him, but he ignored her. "There's something you should know, Erica. I knew Rachel many years ago. When she was a student in college here. She met my father in those days too. But Sara is not, as you imagine, my father's child. She's mine, do you understand? Sara is my daughter!"

CHAPTER NINE

THE silence which greeted Joel's statement had stretched into half a minute when Sara came back into the room. In the normal way, she might have noticed the tension in the atmosphere, but right then all she was concerned about was the stain occupying a prominent place on the front of her new scarlet anorak.

"I've been sick, Mummy," she whispered miserably, tears trickling down her cheeks. "And look what I've done to my an'rak!"

Rachel was unutterably glad of the diversion, although she knew how any child hated being sick. "Oh, darling," she exclaimed, going towards her, "don't worry about it. It'll wash."

"I – I think I've made a mess," Sara continued jerkily. "In – in there." She indicated the hall behind her.

"Oh, my God!" Erica made a gesture of impatience, but Joel silenced her with a look.

"Don't worry about it, poppet," he said, forcing a smile. "Heron will deal with it – "

"I'll deal with it!" essayed Rachel firmly. "If you'll tell me where I can find cleaning materials – "

"I said Heron will deal with it!" Joel's tone was harsh. "Rachel, we have other things to discuss."

"Not now," retorted Rachel, straightening after wiping the tears from Sara's face. "Don't you think you've said enough?"

"I'd second that," remarked Erica dryly, recovering her composure as it became apparent that whatever her previous relationship with Joel might have been, Rachel had obviously little affection for him now. "Joel – "

"Shut up!" Joel staggered across to where Rachel was leading Sara up the steps to the door. "Rachel, where are you going?"

"I should have thought that was obvious. I'm taking Sara home. Good night, Joel. Good night, Miss Grey."

"*Rachel!*"

But Rachel was urging Sara out of the door, and he did not have the strength to prevent them from leaving. Instead, he stood watching them, swaying slightly, and Rachel bolstered her failing determination with the knowledge that Erica would be only too ready to console him after they had gone ...

To her mother's relief, Sara seemed quite recovered from her sickness the following day. The vomiting had probably been due to too much excitement after her earlier inertia, and meeting Erica had not helped. Rachel refused to consider Sara's reactions when she learned that Erica was going to marry her hero. She was bound to be upset, and she hoped and prayed that after these days with Joel the child would react more favourably to James Kingdom. If only he had not had to go away, this situation might never have occurred.

Still, Sara was disposed to accept that for today at least there was no chance of them seeing Joel, and when it was time for her to go to the hospital, she made no fuss. Mrs. Talbot hadn't put in an appearance before they left the flat, but she was waiting for Rachel on her return.

"Sorry I'm late, Mrs. Gilmour," she said apologetically. "But I didn't think you'd mind."

"Not at all." Rachel forced a smile. "It's all a bit silly anyway, isn't it? A grown woman needing a baby-sitter."

Mrs. Talbot coloured. "Oh, I don't think Mr. Kingdom sees it like that, Mrs. Gilmour. But London can be a frightening place to someone who's not used to it."

Rachel was tempted to tell the housekeeper that she had

lived in London for several years at a time when she was a lot more impressionable than she was now, but then decided against it. After all, her track record wasn't that good. She had behaved like a million other foolish girls and got herself pregnant. It was useless telling herself that she had thought her affair was different. No doubt half the other girls would say the same. Women were always fools when it came to their emotions.

The telephone shrilled, and Rachel went to answer it. She had expected it to be James and was surprised to hear Joel's voice. "Rachel? Rachel, is that you?"

"Yes." Rachel glanced awkwardly towards Mrs. Talbot, who was taking her knitting out of her bag and appeared engrossed. "What do you want?"

"I want to see you. Can you come round?"

Rachel gasped. "Sara – "

"Sara's in hospital. I checked. Oh, I know Mrs. Talbot's there, but you're not a prisoner. You can get out."

"I can't – "

"Do you want me to come round there?"

"Don't be silly."

"So?"

Rachel thought desperately. "Are you in bed?"

"No. Would it make a difference if I were?"

"Yes. I shouldn't come."

Joel sounded exasperated. "Well, I'm not. Besides, Heron's here."

"How do I know that?"

"You want to speak to him?"

"No." Rachel sighed and glanced once more at the housekeeper. "What about Erica?"

"Leave Erica to me." He muttered an impatient oath. "Rachel – "

"All right." She drew a deep breath. She would be glad to

get out of the apartment. And Joel was ill. She had nothing to fear. "I'll do it."

"Good."

Joel put down his receiver before she could change her mind and Rachel replaced her receiver carefully. Then she almost jumped out of her skin when it suddenly rang again. Exchanging startled glances with Mrs. Talbot she picked it up. "Yes?"

"Rachel?" It was James's voice, and her knees went weak. "Rachel, where the devil have you been?"

"What do you mean?"

"I've been trying to get you for two nights. Last evening I could get no reply and this evening I've had one no answer and one engaged signal. What's going on?"

"Nothing's going on, James." Rachel was glad he could not see her face. "I – er – last night Sara and I went out for a while. But we were back soon after eight."

"Well, I had a meeting last evening. I couldn't phone after seven-thirty, and by the time it was over, I guessed you'd be in bed."

"I see." Rachel swallowed convulsively. "I'm sorry."

"So where were you this evening?"

"Taking Sara to the hospital, I suppose?"

"Isn't Mrs. Talbot there? Why didn't she answer?"

Rachel sighed. "She was late. I'm sorry if you've had a frustrating time."

"So am I. Just now the phone was engaged. Who were you talking to?"

Rachel couldn't reply. The words stuck in her throat, and he exclaimed: "What is it? Don't you want to tell me?"

Rachel knew she would have to tell him. "Oh, yes, yes," she cried. "It was Joel, if you must know."

"What did he want?" James was curt.

"Oh – this and that."

"That's no answer, Rachel."

"Very well. He wants to see me."

"Why?"

"To – to talk about Sara, I suppose."

"He knows what's really wrong with her, doesn't he?"

"I – well, yes."

"I'm glad you've been honest about that, Rachel because I've spoken to Joel myself, and I *know* he knows."

"I see." Rachel's hand holding the receiver shook a little.

"Why did you tell him?"

"I – I didn't. He – found out."

"From Sara? When he took her to his apartment?"

Rachel gasped. "In a – manner of speaking."

"I know all about it, you see, Rachel. There's no point in lying to me."

"I'm not lying to you."

"You'd better not."

"James, what is this? Why are you speaking like this?"

"I want to know what Joel's been saying to you. How you mean to behave when this is all over?"

"What do you mean?"

"You must know Joel wants to adopt the child."

"*Adopt – Sara?*" Rachel caught her breath. "No, I don't know that."

"Perhaps that's what he wants to talk to you about."

Rachel rubbed a confused hand across her cheek. "But – but – "

"You should never have told Joel that Sara was his daughter."

"Perhaps – perhaps I shouldn't . . ."

"Do you want him to have the child?"

Rachel almost choked. "You know I don't!" She tried to think coherently. "James, I love Sara – "

"I know you do. I'm quite fond of her myself. But it's only

fair that you should know what Joel is thinking."

"Yes. Yes, well, you needn't worry, James. No one is going to take Sara away from me. The operation will go ahead, as planned, and we'll be married just as soon as you're recovered."

There was a moment's silence, and then James said slowly: "I've been thinking about that, Rachel. About our marriage, I mean. Bearing in mind Joel's intentions, don't you think it might be a good idea to get married before Sara has the transplant –"

"*Before?*"

"Yes, before." James hesitated. "Rachel, if we were married, if I had legally adopted Sara as my child, no one could take her away from you – from us."

Rachel pressed a hand to her churning stomach. "I don't know, James ..."

"Why not? What difference does it make? Once we were married I could go into hospital, Sara and I could have the necessary treatment, and afterwards there would be nothing to delay us in this country."

Rachel didn't know how to reply. Her head was spinning. She was totally confused and disturbed. "James, I have to think –"

"Do you?" He sounded impatient. "Why? Were you thinking of changing your mind after the deed was done?"

"*No!*" Rachel was indignant. "I – I wouldn't do that."

"Very well, then."

"Oh, James, please – give me a couple of days to think it over. It's so unexpected – so sudden!"

He was silent again, and then he said: "I'm coming home in three days, Rachel. Will you give me your answer then?"

Rachel breathed an unknowing sigh of relief. "Oh, yes – yes." She licked dry lips. "You're not – angry, are you, James?"

James snorted. "I'm not angry, no. Disappointed, perhaps.

Just remember, you have as much to gain from this as I have. Once you were my wife, no one could take Sara away from you!"

After he had rung off, Rachel turned to the housekeeper. "I'm – er – I'm going out for a little while, Mrs. Talbot. You don't mind, do you?"

Mrs. Talbot looked doubtful. "Going out, Mrs. Gilmour?"

"Yes." Rachel nodded. "Er – Mr. Kingdom knows about it."

Now why had she said that? she asked herself impatiently. She was not a child, to have to explain her movements. Was this to be her role in future, though? Always having to find excuses for doing what she wanted to do?

"Well, if you're sure, Mrs. Gilmour. But it is late, you know. After nine."

"I know, I know." Rachel walked through to her bedroom and pulled her suede jacket on over the red velvet waistcoat and trousers she was wearing. The navy blue shirt she was wearing with the suit was not very warm to go out in, but she intended hiring a taxi at the end of the close. And besides, she didn't expect she would be taking off her coat at Joel's apartment.

The taxi deposited her outside Breton Towers, and the lift transported her smoothly to the penthouse floor. She rang Joel's bell and waited. But it was not Heron who opened the door to her, as she had expected, but Joel himself, dark and disturbing, in cream suede pants and a fine black woollen sweater. He stood back politely when he saw her, and said: "Won't you come in?"

Rachel glanced up at him dubiously as she did so. Much of the strain of the night before had been wiped from his face, and only his eyes reflected a rawness of the pain he had suffered. But he was obviously recovered, and she kicked herself for not asking him this on the telephone.

"You're better," she remarked flatly, halting above the steps leading down into the body of the room. Tonight it was lamplit, the blinds drawn back to reveal a panorama of the lights of London below. "Why didn't you tell me? We could have arranged to meet elsewhere."

"Why?" Joel went lithely past her and down the steps. "This is as good a place as any." He looked back over his shoulder. "Take off your coat and come and sit down. What will you drink?"

Rachel shook her head. "What is it you want to say to me, Joel?" she demanded. "Let's get it over and done with, shall we?"

Joel halted by a trolley laden with bottles and glasses. "There's only you and I here, Rachel," he said quietly. "There's no hurry."

Rachel's eyes widened and she glanced towards the door as if measuring the distance. "I thought you told me Heron was here!" she exclaimed.

Joel sighed. "All right, so he is. But he's in his own rooms. To all intents and purposes we're alone. Does that satisfy you?"

Rachel remained where she was, thrusting her hands deep into the pockets of her jacket. "I don't think there's any point in dragging this out, Joel," she declared. "Your father rang me this evening and told me he'd been speaking to you."

"Rachel, for God's sake, come and sit down!" Joel stared at her grimly. "I'm not about to seduce you or rape you or do any of the things your agile imagination is summoning up. I just want to talk. *Talk* – that's all."

Rachel's breathing quickened. "What about?"

"Come and sit down, and I'll tell you."

Half reluctantly, Rachel came down the steps and perched on the edge of the couch. She didn't take off her coat and when he held out a glass of colourless liquid she had to take her hand out of her pocket to take it. "Wh-what's this?"

"Dry Martini and soda. That is innocuous enough for you, isn't it?"

Rachel nodded, taking the glass. "Thank you."

Joel went back and poured himself some whisky and then came to join her on the couch, lounging back in his seat, nearer than she would have preferred. "Now, what did my father tell you?"

Rachel shrugged awkwardly. "Just – just that you – had been talking to him."

Joel's expression was scathing. "Just that and nothing more? He rang just to tell you he had been speaking to me!"

"No, of course not." Rachel coloured. "He – he had other things to say."

"Such as what?"

"I don't have to tell you that."

Joel sounded scornful. "Did he tell you I'd spoken to the surgeon who is to perform the operation?"

"No." Rachel shook her head. "Why – why did you speak to Mr. Lorrimer?"

"I wanted to know the facts." Joel drew up one knee, resting his outstretched arm upon it, studying the liquid in his glass. "It's not going to work, you know."

"What's not going to work?" Rachel felt a tightening of her stomach muscles. "What are you talking about?"

"The transplant. I don't like it."

"What don't you like?" Rachel's face was a little paler now.

"Oh, don't look so concerned. If anyone can do it, Lorrimer can, I'll grant you that." He sighed. "It's not that. It's the effects – afterwards."

"What do you mean?" Rachel stared at him.

Joel shook his head. "Look, Sara is a child, right?"

"That doesn't make any difference. I asked that –"

"Let me finish!" Joel paused, and then went on: "As I said,

Sara is a child. The problems she's had this far have – well, retarded her physical growth slightly, haven't they?" Rachel reluctantly nodded and he continued: "All right. Fortunately the effects have been minimal so far. But if the transplant takes place – the transplant of an adult kidney, healthy or otherwise – she's going to need some kind of suppressive drugs to survive. And you know what suppressive drugs do, don't you? They stunt growth!"

"I don't believe you." Rachel was chilled. "Mr. Lorrimer said there was every chance that the operation would be successful."

"It probably will be. Technically, at least. But ring Lorrimer if you don't believe what I say. Ask him to explain it again. He's already explained these things, both to you and my father, but I guess your main concern was that Sara should survive the operation. I don't think you've thought about afterwards, have you? Well, I'm not happy about it."

"You're not happy about it!" she echoed unsteadily. "How do you think I feel? What you're forgetting is that Sara can't survive on the machine for the rest of her life. Oh, I know great advances have been made, and she could live for years... But that's not a satisfactory solution, is it? I want her to have the chance to lead a normal life."

"So do I!"

"Oh, yes? Is that why you're telling me these things? Why you're trying to frighten me into calling off the transplant?"

"I'm not trying to frighten you, Rachel. For God's sake, all I'm suggesting is that – well, perhaps you shouldn't rush into this. Sara has adapted herself to the machine – she's not dying or anything. As you say, great biological advances have been made during the past few years. Maybe there are even greater advances to be made in the future. Perhaps you should wait a while and consider. Rachel, I want what's best for the child, too, you know!"

"Do you? *Do you?*" Rachel thrust the glass she was holding on to a side table and got to her feet. "Why? Why? So you can take her away from me?"

"What the hell are you talking about?"

Joel rose now, but Rachel backed away from him. "Don't try to deny it. You father told me what your have in mind."

"Which is?" Joel's voice was icily cold.

"Adoption!" Rachel's lips moved bitterly. "You want to adopt Sara. That was what you threatened to do in the beginning, wasn't it? When you first discovered that you had a daughter! What an arrogant swine you are!"

Joel finished his whisky and dropped the empty glass carelessly on the carpet. "So that's what he told you, did he?"

"Do you deny it?"

Joel shrugged. "Would it make any difference if I did?"

"What's that supposed to mean?"

Joel shook his head. "No. I don't deny that I want to adopt Sara – "

"That's crazy!" Rachel spoke distractedly.

"Why is it crazy?"

"You don't even *like* children!"

"On the contrary, I like Sara very much."

Rachel moved her head confusedly. "But you always said – "

"I know what I always said. And I used to believe it, too. But not any longer. Success that comes too easily is no challenge. I've been a fool, Rachel. You don't know how much of a fool!"

Rachel put up a hand to her forehead. Her head was aching dully and she felt sick. "I – I won't let you do it!" she cried, and his expression became a little cruel.

"Won't you? How will you stop me?"

"By marrying your father."

"Is that what he said?" Joel asked contemptuously.

"What if it is?"

He shook his head. "Oh, Rachel, now who's the fool?"

"Don't you dare to call me a fool!" she stormed, her breast heaving. "Oh, why did I ever allow myself to become involved with this family?"

"Because you loved me," replied Joel, stepping close to her so that when she automatically backed away she came up against the wall behind her. She tried to twist away from him, but he was too quick for her and his fingers slid round her throat. "You love me now, if you'd only admit it."

"You? *You*?" Rachel forced a scornful laugh. "I *hate* you!"

Joel's fingers tightened, his thumbs massaging the vulnerable muscles that surrounded her windpipe. "Have a care, Rachel," he advised her, his eyes narrowed to slits between the thick lashes. "Don't tempt me to do what I wanted to do to you when you disappeared six years ago."

The tension in Rachel's body snapped, and she went weak, swaying against him. It had all been too much for her and she no longer felt capable of making any decision.

"Let me go, Joel," she begged wearily, her face pressed against his chest. "Please – I can't take any more!"

Joel's hands were unsteady as they slid the suede jacket from her shoulders and it fell unheeded to the floor. He gathered her closely against him, his hands moving possessively over her back, fitting her body into his so that she could feel him trembjing, too. He kissed her then, hot passionate kisses that aroused an answering passion inside her which she was not strong enough to resist.

"I don't want to hurt you, Rachel," he muttered, against her mouth, his breath mingling with hers. "I just want to love you. Let me love you, Rachel. Stay with me . . ."

But it was those words which brought Rachel to her senses. What was she doing, she thought hysterically, allowing him to touch her like this? Kissing him with an abandonment that invited everything she got! He wanted to love her, she didn't doubt it. It was his way of saying he wanted to make love to her. But making love and loving were two vastly different things. And while her senses cried out for his possession, ached with the memory of that unforgettable night they had spent together, she had to remember the outcome of that folly and what he was trying to take from her now.

Tearing herself out of his arms, she faced him, shaking uncontrollably. "Oh, yes, you'd do that, wouldn't you?" she accused emotively. "Sleep with me and then tell James what you'd done! What a victory that would have been, wouldn't it? How would it have sounded in a courtroom preferring custody of the child? Is that what you think? What would you say? That the mother is a loose woman – engaged to one man and having an affair with another – "

"Rachel, you're talking nonsense!" he grated. "For God's sake, let me explain – "

"I don't want your explanations, Joel!"

"*Rachel!* Come here!"

He tried to take hold of her, but she eluded him, darting up the steps and out of the door before he could stop her. She heard him coming behind her and instead of waiting for the lift she began to run down the stairs. Round and round, down and down, her head was spinning, and her legs ached. Was he following her? Had he taken the lift? Would he be waiting for her at the bottom? The stairs seemed endless. How many floors, how many more flights? She didn't think she could go much further. The stairs seemed to be behaving in a most peculiar way, was she climbing the stairs, or descending them. Surely they were going up ahead of her. She put out her foot to mount the first stair, but there was nothing there, and she was falling, falling, bumping her arms and legs – oh, the pain! And then oblivion ...

CHAPTER TEN

RACHEL opened her lids to a brilliant light that hurt her eyes. She didn't know where she was. The ceiling above her was plain and emulsioned in white, and there seemed to be whiteness all around her. It was that that hurt her eyes.

She blinked and became aware of a throbbing behind her temples, and various aches and pains throughout her body. When she tried to move, she couldn't. She was lying in a narrow bed, and the bedclothes were so tight she couldn't move.

Panic rose inside her, but before it could manifest itself a face interposed between her and the brilliant white wall ahead of her.

"Now then, Mrs. Gilmour," said a gentle, feminine voice. "How do you feel?"

Rachel tried to focus on the smiling face, but it was difficult. She didn't know that face, and what was it on the woman's head? A cap? A nurse's cap! *A nurse's cap!*

"Sara!" she cried in agonised tones. "Where's Sara?"

"Sara is perfectly all right," the nurse assured her firmly. "It's you we've been worried about."

Rachel closed her eyes again. A tremendous drowsiness was sweeping over her again, and she hadn't the strength to fight it. "Sara," she said again, desperately. "Sara . . ."

The next time she opened her eyes, the walls didn't seem quite so white, but perhaps that was because it was daylight outside. She frowned, trying to think. What was she doing here? If this was a hospital why was she in it? But her effort to think made her head hurt.

"Mrs. Gilmour?"

The voice was masculine this time, the face older, more lined. Rachel swallowed convulsively. "I – what am I doing here?"

The man in the white coat gestured to a nurse behind him, and she came forward to trickle some liquid between Rachel's lips. It was cool, and it felt good.

"Now, Mrs. Gilmour," said the man, "I don't want you to talk. Just relax. You're going to be all right."

"Why – where am I?"

"You're in hospital, my dear. Don't you remember falling downstairs?"

Rachel's brows drew together. Falling downstairs? *Falling downstairs?* She drew an unsteady breath. *Joel! The apartment!*

"Sara," she breathed unsteadily. "Where is Sara?"

"Sara is fine, fine."

"I want to see her. Where is she?"

"You mustn't excite yourself, Mrs. Gilmour," said the man sternly, drawing back the covers to lift her wrist. "You're not allowed any visitors right now. You'll see Sara, all in good time."

"She'll worry – Who's looking after her?"

"I understand her father has taken charge of her," replied the man firmly. "Now, I'm just going to – "

But Rachel wasn't listening. *Her father! Joel! The apartment!* She tried to move, but couldn't, and tears came to her eyes. The pain in her head was increasing. Oh, God, what was wrong with her? Why couldn't she move? Was she paralysed? She had to think ... to think ... But thinking was so painful. The man's face was blurring, when he let go of her wrist her arm fell limply on to the sheet. If she could just lift it again ... Blackness was edging the limits of her vision. She had to ask, she must ask somebody ...

Her eyes flickered. Someone was sitting beside the bed. But that wasn't possible. Where had the man in the white coat gone – and the nurse . . . ? The man sitting beside the bed didn't wear a white coat. He was wearing a white shirt and a suede jacket. He was hunched in a sort of exhausted position, but she could feel her fingers lying in his. She moved her fingers experimentally. Relief flooded through her. She could actually move her fingers . . .

The movement had disturbed the man and he lifted his head to stare searchingly at her. It was Joel. She knew that at once, even though he looked haggard and drawn, a blue shadow of beard darkening his jawline. She blinked again. The only light in the room was coming from a lamp beside the bed. It was night again. She must have slept all day!

"Rachel?" he breathed unsteadily, leaning towards her. "Rachel, are you awake?"

She flexed her lips. "I – I think so." Then a terrible thought struck her. If Joel was here . . . "Joel, where – where's Sara?"

He straightened his shoulders wearily, taking her hand in both of his. "Cool it, honey," he advised, stroking the veins of her wrist. "Sara's being taken care of. All you've got to think about is getting better."

"When can I see her?"

"Soon. Soon."

Rachel shifted restlessly, and as she did so she felt something that seemed to be bound about her head. Frowning slightly, she lifted her free arm and probed her scalp. It was swathed in bandages, and she could feel none of the hair that used to flow so freely about her shoulders when she was in bed. The probing made her realise how tender her scalp felt and she turned horrified eyes in Joel's direction. "What – what am I – wearing a – a bandage for?"

"Don't you remember?" he asked, shaking his head, his eyes amazingly tender.

"I – I know I fell downstairs. I – I remember hurting my arms and legs . . ."

Joel lifted her hand to his lips and pressed his face to her palm. "It was my fault," he muttered in a harsh voice. "Mine! You were running away from me! Oh, Rachel, I've been out of my mind these past days!"

"D-days?" Rachel tried to understand him. "Wh-what do you mean?"

"Rachel, you've been lying here almost a week!"

"A – week!" Rachel gasped. "But – but – "

"Don't try to talk." Joel stretched out a hand and stroked a finger across her lips. "I must tell someone you're awake."

He half rose, but Rachel held on to his hand tightly. "Not yet. Joel. Please – how can I have been here that long? I – I don't remember . . ."

Joel sighed, sinking back into his chair. "You were unconscious for several days. Rachel. Then – then you were operated upon."

"My head!" Rachel gasped. "They operated on my head, didn't they? Have they shaved off my hair?"

She was getting distressed and he soothed her firmly. "Rachel, let me get the doctor – "

"No, no!" She almost sobbed the words. "They did, didn't they? Answer me! They shaved my head!"

"They had to, Rachel. There was bleeding inside . . ." He sighed heavily. "You're going to be all right now. Your hair will grow again, just as beautiful as ever."

Tears flowed down her cheeks, and he dragged himself away from her and went in search of assistance. When the doctor and the nursing Sister appeared, Joel was not with them.

During the next twenty-four hours, Rachel learned to accept that she had had a very lucky escape from death, and that a shaved head was a small price to pay compared to the paralysis the cerebral haemorrhage had caused. She felt terribly weak and listless, but at least she could move, if very slowly, and the pain in her head was bearable. She asked about Sara, of course, when she could see her, and where she was staying, but the answers she received were frustratingly vague, and she was still not strong enough to assert herself.

A further two days made a lot of difference. She was eating something now, whereas at first food had nauseated her, and her strength was slowly returning. She could talk, without getting too tired, and propped on her pillows she enjoyed looking at the hospital gardens through the long windows.

"When will I be able to see Sara?" she demanded of the doctor, the next time he came to examine her, and he regarded her with a certain amount of consideration before replying:

"You can't see her yet, Mrs. Gilmour. Because Sara is in hospital, too."

"You mean – for her treatment?"

"No. Not for her treatment. She's had the operation you wanted her to have."

"What?" Rachel stared at him disbelievingly. "Wh-what are you saying?"

"Sara had a kidney transplant a week ago, and I believe it to be a complete success."

"A – a – week – ago?" Rachel couldn't take it in.

"Now don't go getting upset about it. You've got nothing to worry about. She's in expert hands, believe me."

"But how could she have the operation? When – when I was not there? Who gave permission?"

"I understand, in certain circumstances where previous permission has been given, the operation is permitted to go ahead. Besides," he paused, "wouldn't her father have that right?"

Rachel turned her face into the pillow. "So – so Mr. Kingdom is back from Germany," she choked.

"Mr. Kingdom?" the doctor looked surprised. "I didn't know he was going to Germany."

Rachel turned to look at him and then sighed. Of course, he thought she meant *Joel* Kingdom. "It doesn't matter," she said dully. Then she forced herself to an awareness of what this would mean to Sara. "And – and you say – it's successful? I – I can't believe it."

"That's natural." The doctor smiled. "I can understand how you feel, but sometimes it's best that these things are done like that – on the spur of the moment, so to speak. Your little girl has been very lucky, Mrs. Gilmour. She's got every opportunity now to lead a normal life."

"Yes."

Rachel pressed her lips together. So it was done. And she could guess who was behind it. James Kingdom. Perhaps Joel had revealed his doubts to his father, perhaps James had been afraid that she, Rachel, might share them. And wasn't it also true that she had – deep down? Wasn't that half the frustration she had felt with Joel? Hadn't he voiced her fears she had had all along?

But that was the past now. Sara had had the transplant. She was recovering. It was a success – the doctor had said so. Perhaps it would be all right, after all. And certainly now James would see that Joel had no opportunity to claim his daughter. Why then did the knowledge bring her no pleasure?

During the next few days she half expected Joel to contact her. Surely he would know how she was feeling about Sara, might take compassion on her and come and tell her how Sara was really feeling – how she had reacted to this prolonged separation from her mother. But he did not appear, and when her first visitor was announced she was astounded to see Erica Grey. Dressed in a slim-fitting suit of soft black crêpe, and carrying a sheaf of roses and carnations, Erica looked coolly elegant, entering the austere hospital room with the self-possession of a fashion model. Only Rachel felt that her black suit was an apt choice. Erica had the warmth of a hungry tarantula.

"Hello, Rachel," she mouthed, for the nurse's benefit, laying the sheaf of flowers on the bed. "How are you?"

"I'm recovering, thank you." Rachel dismissed the nurse, who had escorted the visitor, with a slight nod. "Why have you come, Erica?"

Erica raised her dark eyebrows. "May I sit down?"

"If you must."

"I do." Erica seated herself comfortably, crossing one slender leg over the other. "Er – I should tell you, shouldn't I? Joel asked me to come."

Rachel's nerves tightened. "Oh, yes?"

"Yes." Erica smoothed her skirt with a gloved hand. "He – he hasn't the time – he's been working, you know. But he wanted you to know that we hadn't forgotten you – or Sara."

"Sara?" Rachel couldn't prevent the automatic response.

"Yes, Sara." Erica smiled, but it didn't reach her eyes. "You know, of course, that she's had her operation?"

"Of course."

"Joel arranged it."

"*Joel!*"

"Why, yes. Didn't you know?"

"No." Rachel plucked nervously at the coverlet. "I – have you seen her?"

"Naturally. Joel sees her every day and I go with him whenever I can. Oh, dear . . ." She pressed a hand to her mouth as though she shouldn't have said what she had, but Rachel knew every word had been deliberate. "Joel – makes a special effort to see his daughter, of course. You – well, you're rather different, aren't you?"

It took a great effort for Rachel to keep her voice steady,

as she asked: "Why did you come here, Miss Grey? What is it you're trying to say to me?"

"I've told you. Joel asked me to come."

"Why? He knows I wouldn't care whether he came or not."

"Ah, but is that true?" Erica's eyes were calculating. "You and I know better than that, don't we – *Mrs.* Gilmour?"

"I don't know what you mean."

"I think you do. You might be able to pretend to yourself that you don't care what happens to Joel, but you can't pretend to me! You see, you and I share the same disease, and I know the symptoms."

Rachel took a deep breath. The strength she had would not stand this kind of verbal skirmishing for very long. "You're – mistaken, Miss Grey. I feel nothing for Joel but contempt. You're welcome to him."

Erica put the tips of her fingers together. "And Sara?"

"What about Sara?"

"You want to keep her, don't you?"

"Of course."

"Then marry James Kingdom, Mrs. Gilmour. Before you lose her altogether."

Rachel stared at her curiously. "Why should you care?"

"Can't you guess? I don't care for children, Mrs. Gilmour. They're not my scene. The thought of caring for a child in sickness and in health does not appeal to me at all. However, if Joel is determined to adopt Sara ..." She tipped her head on one side. "Do you understand?"

"But he won't – *he can't.*"

"I shouldn't be too sure of that. Things can change very rapidly in a child's life. It's obvious that she cares about Joel, and I don't have to tell you that he cares about her. Can you honestly compete when it comes to what both of you can do for the child?"

Rachel bent her head. "There's no question of Joel adopting

Sara. I'm going to marry James Kingdom just as soon as he's up and about again."

"*James?* Up and about again?" Now it was Erica's turn to look confused. "What are you talking about?"

Rachel pressed herself back against the pillows. A little niggling pain was beginning near her temples and she wished Erica would just go and leave her alone. It was all too much for her. She must have gone a shade paler because Erica sat up in her chair, and said: "Rachel? Rachel, are you all right?"

When Rachel recovered consciousness, Sister Thomas was standing looking down at her. "Well, Mrs. Gilmour," she exclaimed, half reprovingly, as Rachel opened her eyes. "You do like giving us shocks, don't you?"

"I'm sorry."

Sister Thomas sighed impatiently. "I told Nurse Harper that Miss Grey wasn't to stay longer than five minutes." She shook her head. "How are you feeling?"

Rachel put up a hand to her forehead. "Just – a little dizzy," she confessed.

Sister Thomas clicked her tongue. "If I'd known Miss Grey was going to upset you like this, I should't have allowed her to see you at all."

Rachel struggled to look round. "Miss Grey? Wh-where is she?"

"She left. I wasn't sorry. But she left you these." She held up the sheaf of roses and carnations. "I'll have Nurse Harper put them in water for you."

"No!" Rachel spoke urgently. "No, don't do that, Sister. I – take them away. Give them to somebody else. Keep them, if you want to. I don't want them."

Sister Thomas frowned suspiciously. "Mrs. Gilmour, I thought Miss Grey said she was a friend of yours?"

Rachel shifted restlessly, as the dizziness receded. "she's an – acquaintance, that's all. Oh, please – just take the flowers away. I never want to see them again."

During the next few days Rachel's physical condition improved at almost the same rate as her mental state deteriorated. She expected James daily to come and see her, knowing that as soon as he was discharged from the hospital he would appear. Casual questioning of the nurse who attended her had disclosed that the donor in a kidney transplant was generally able to leave hospital within two weeks of the operation. Rachel was desperate to see Sara, but his hospital – Lady Margaret's – was some distance from St. Matthew's, and she had to resign herself to the fact that they would not see one another until Sara was up and about again. But when she was capable of putting pen to paper, Rachel wrote to her daughter and received a note back again, obviously written by a nurse.

"*Dear Mummy,*" she read, "*I was sorry to hear that you had been poorly, too, and I miss you terribly. But Joel has been to see me, and he told me that you were getting better. Mr. Kingdom has been to see me, too, but I . . .*"

Then what had been written had been scribbled over, but Rachel could still make out the words *don't like him.* She sighed, and continued:

"*. . . don't think he is as nice as Joel.*" Sara wouldn't! "*Doctor Lorrimer says I shall soon be able to go out and when I can I will come and see you. Lots of love, Sara.*"

Rachel felt the hot sting of tears behind her eyes as she re-read the letter. Had James said anything to Sara about their forthcoming marriage? Had he told her that without Rachel's accident, they might well have been married by now? Was that why Sara had said she didn't like him?

Rachel pushed the letter back into its envelope. Well, if James had been to see Sara, it would not be long before he came to see her. And then . . .

The following afternoon Sister Thomas came into her room

looking rather thoughtful. "You have another visitor, Mrs. Gilmour," she said reluctantly. "Mr. Kingdom. Do you want to see him?"

"Oh! Oh, yes! That is – " Rachel put up a hand to her bandaged head. "Do – do I look an awful mess?"

Sister Thomas gave her a reproving smile. "I gather Mr. Kingdom's opinion is important to you. I don't blame you. He's a very attractive man. Half my nurses made fools of themselves the last time he was here."

Rachel's lips parted. "Wait!" This as Sister Thomas walked to the door. "Wait a minute!" She hesitated. "Sister Thomas, Mr. Kingdom – he – he's a young man?"

Sister Thomas frowned. "Don't you know?"

Rachel nodded quickly. "Yes. Yes, of course. But there are two." She plucked at the bedcover. "Did – did he give his name? His Christian name?"

"He didn't have to. I already know it. Joel Kingdom is not unknown in art appreciation circles."

"Oh! Oh, I see." Rachel trembled. Then: "I don't want to see him, Sister. Please ask him to go away."

"To go away, Mrs. Gilmour?" Sister Thomas was amazed. "But, Mrs. Gilmour, Mr. Kingdom was responsible for bringing you here, for providing you with the best attention possible. Mr. Frazer – " she mentioned the name of the surgeon who had operated on Rachel, " – Mr. Frazer is the foremost specialist in inter-cranium surgery. Mr. Kingdom arranged all this and then stayed in the hospital day and night until you came round from the operation! Don't you think you owe him something?"

Rachel refused to look at her. "I'm sorry, but I don't want to see him."

"But, Mrs. Gilmour – "

Rachel looked up then, hectic colour splashing her cheeks, her eyes unnaturally bright. "Do I have to see him?" she demanded. "Is that a ruling here?"

Sister Thomas sighed. "You know it's not." She shook her head. "Well, if you won't change your mind!"

"I won't." Rachel watched the Sister move towards the door again. "I – Sister! Tell him – tell him I'm very grateful – for all he's done, but it's no use. We have nothing to say to one another."

She half thought that Joel would not accept it, that he would be angry and come bursting into the room demanding to know what was going on. But he didn't, and contrarily she wanted to cry. Then she chided herself. What was the matter with her, for heaven's sake? Joel had made his position clear enough. James and Erica had made Joel's position clear enough. His determination was to take Sara away from her, and only James offered an alternative. An alternative she was already bound to take.

Joel tried to see Rachel three times during the next week, but without success. Each time she turned him away, Rachel felt as if she was turning away a part of herself, and this knowledge filled her with despair. Since Erica's visit, she had determinedly tried not to think about Joel in any way except as the man who was trying to take Sara from her, but deep inside, the agony she suffered had little to do with the child. Every poignant tune on the radio, the stirring evidence of nature at work in the flower-strewn gardens beyond her windows, made her acutely aware of the emotions she was so futilely trying to deny. She should have had the sense to realise, she told herself fiercely, that an intimate association with the man she had loved desperately – *the father of her child* – would have disastrous consequences. She had never stopped loving him, that was the trouble, and she bitterly despised her foolishness. The sooner James married her and took her out of Joel's orbit, the better ...

She was overwhelmingly relieved therefore when Sister

Thomas announced a couple of days later that a Mr. James Kingdom would like to see her. Rachel was out of bed now, sitting in a chair by the window, reading, and she looked up eagerly, putting a nervous hand to her bandages.

"I – I'll see him," she said, nodding. "Show him in."

James looked amazingly unchanged. She had expected the operation to have had some effect on him, but it didn't appear to have made the slightest difference. He was just as tall and erect as ever, businesslike in his grey City suit. He came into her room slowly, appraising her slender figure in the soft blue dressing gown, fixing his eyes on her pale face.

"Well, Rachel?" he said, shaking his head as he laid a bouquet of white roses across her knees. "What have you been doing to yourself?"

He didn't attempt to kiss her, and she was glad, indicating the chair opposite hers, urging him to sit down. He did so and she looked down at the roses, glad of the diversion. "They're – they're beautiful!" she exclaimed.

James regarded her curiously. "How are you, Rachel?"

"Oh!" She looked up. "I'm – I'm fine. Much better. Mr. Frazer says I'll be able to go home in a few days."

"Will you?" James sounded surprised. "And who will look after you?"

Rachel flushed. "I'll manage."

"Have you seen Sara?"

"No. Not yet. But I expect I will soon." She paused, licking her lips. "James – James, I haven't thanked you yet..."

"Thanked me?" He frowned.

"Of course." She moved her shoulders awkwardly. "For – for going ahead with the operation, I mean. My being in hospital has delayed everything else, hasn't it? I – I'm sorry."

James continued to regard her steadily for several disconcerting minutes, and then he said: "You – haven't seen Joel."

Rachel shook her head. "Not – not since – not since the night I had the operation. I – I understand he brought me here."

"Yes. Yes, he did." James frowned. "What were you doing running down the stairs of his apartment building?"

"Hasn't he told you?" Rachel uttered a short laugh. "No – no, of course, he hasn't, or you wouldn't be asking, would you? I – we – we had a row over – over Joel wanting to adopt Sara."

"He still intends to do that."

"I know, I know." Rachel pressed her lips together. "But – but you won't let that happen now, will you, James?" She twisted the stem of a long delicate bloom. "You – you promised me that . . ."

She broke off and James seemed to mentally shake himself as he leaned forward and took one of her hands. "You mean you want us to get married as soon as possible?"

Rachel nodded. "That was what we – what we arranged, wasn't it?"

"Indeed." James took a deep breath. "Indeed it was."

"I want to get it done and over with. I want Sara to have a proper home and parents. You can give her that, James."

James got to his feet, pacing throughtfully about the room. "I suppose it's possible for us to be married here – in the hospital," he commented slowly. "It could be – arranged."

"In the hospital?" Rachel put probing fingers to her lips. "Oh, but I look such a mess!"

James' expression was wry. "I hardly see how that matters. If it's what you want . . ."

Rachel tried to think coherently. Once she and James were married, there would be no turning back. It was a terrifying thought. But if she wanted to keep Sara . . .

"All – all right," she agreed jerkily. "If – it you can arrange it."

"Oh, I'll arrange it," asserted James, with a little of the arrogance she was used to from him. Really, he was being very understanding with her today. Not at all the way she had expected him to behave after going ahead with the operation.

"You – you've seen Sara," she put in, trying to concentrate on the child and not on her own feelings. "How – how is she?"

James studied her intently for several moments as though trying to gauge her motives for asking, and then answered: "She's very well. The transplant was a huge success."

Rachel felt weak. "I'm so glad. Is she – when will she be able to come and see me?"

James gave her another of those austere looks. "Soon – soon." He hesitated. "I'll arrange for – Mrs. Talbot to stay at the flat and look after her."

"Oh, will you? That would be thoughtful. At least she knows Mrs. Talbot. I can't wait to see her, though. It's been ... so long ..."

"Yes." James came back to his chair and sat down again, studying her once more. "Rachel." He took her hand in his again. "Rachel, I want you to promise me something."

"Yes?" She looked doubtfully at him.

"Yes." He paused. "I want you to promise me that if Joel tries to see you, you'll continue to refuse to see him."

"You – *know* – about that?" Rachel was confused.

"Of course." James sounded impatient. "I've seen Joel, Rachel. Several times."

"Of course," she echoed softly. "That was silly, wasn't it?" She looked up at him. "All right, if that's your decision."

"It is. I don't want him – upsetting you. I think he's done enough, one way and the other."

Rachel could have said "So do I", but she didn't.

Nevertheless, the next two days were nerve-racking. At times she dreaded Joel appearing and confronting her with her intentions, and at others she found herself worrying in case Sara was going to be hurt by being forcibly separated from the man she had obviously grown to care for. Perhaps she, Rachel, was the selfish one, denying their daughter the right to choose. Was she so afraid that Sara might choose to stay with her father? Oughtn't she to be given that chance anyway? Rachel's obligation to James Kingdom was not consequent upon Sara's accompanying them to Greece. He had played his part and just because Rachel was now being called upon to play hers did not mean that Sara was bound to go with them. Wasn't she in fact using Sara to make her own life more bearable with a man she did not love?

And then, on that second afternoon, she had another visitor.

The previous day the doctor had removed the bandages from Rachel's head, and left only a heavy plaster to cover the wound he had inflicted. But her growing hair was still just a covering of silvery fluff on her scalp, and so they had provided her with a matching wig in a shoulder-length pageboy style. It looked all right, but Rachel was terribly self-conscious and hadn't yet summoned up enough courage to wear it. She thought she had looked more like herself with the bandages swathing her head.

Sister Thomas looked rather pleased with herself when she told Rachel about her visitor. "It's someone you're sure to want to see," she assured her indulgently, handing her the wig and a hand mirror to see her reflection as she put it on.

Rachel fumbled with the fastening and surveyed herself without liking. "Who is it?" she demanded, handing Sister Thomas the mirror again. "Not – not Joel Kingdom?"

"No." Sister Thomas shook her head. "Wait a minute. I'll get her for you."

And before Rachel could protest that she hadn't yet said she would see the visitor, she left the room, returning a few seconds later with a small bouncing figure in red dungarees and a white tee-shirt, straight dark hair swinging about her small excited face.

"Sara!" Rachel could hardly believe her eyes, but she met her daughter halfway, gathering her into her arms. "Oh, Sara!" half tearfully. "You don't know how good it is to see you again!"

Sister Thomas tactfully withdrew and for several minutes they remained close to one another, exchanging the kind of greetings that all children reserve for their parents. But at last Rachel drew Sara towards a chair and sitting down, pulled the child on to her knee.

"You look fine!" she exclaimed unsteadily. "How do you feel?"

"I feel all right," replied Sara indifferently, shrugging her shoulders. "And I don't have to use that machine any more."

"No, I know." Rachel moved her head helplessly. "Oh, Sara, I have missed you."

"I missed you, too," admitted Sara, stroking her cheek. "But everyone's been ever so kind to me. I've got lots of new toys and games! Joel brought me heaps of things. He said some of them were from you."

"Did he?" Rachel's heart gave a lurch. Controlling the tremor in her voice, she added: "And you saw Uncle James, too, didn't you?"

Sara wrinkled her nose. "Oh, yes. But he just brought me a musical box, from Germany."

"Oh, Sara! You don't judge people by what they bring you!"

"I know. But Joel says he loves me. He says he wants me to be his little girl!"

Rachel's stomach muscles tightened sickeningly. "And – and what did Uncle James say?"

"I don't remember." Sara pursed her lips. "I don't like that man!"

"Sara!" Rachel shook her a little. "Don't say things like that. Besides, Uncle James couldn't come and see you as often as Joel. He's been in hospital, too, remember?"

"Why?" Sara stared at her.

"You know. Uncle James gave you one of his kidneys so that you could get properly better!"

"No, he didn't." Sara was disconcertingly assured. "It was that little boy – the one who died."

Rachel was wholly confused. "What little boy who died?"

"The boy who was knocked down by that car." Sara shook her head. "It was terribly sad. But Dr. Lorrimer said that God made these decisions, not doctors."

Rachel couldn't take it in. "Sara, what are you talking about?"

Sara gave an exasperated sigh. "Don't you know anything, Mummy? I've just 'splained! A little boy was knocked down, near the hospital, the night you had your accident. Joel said the doctors looked everywhere for you, but not in a hospital!" She giggled.

Rachel felt a dawning comprehension. "You mean – you mean you got one of this little boy's kidneys?"

"That's just what I said!" exclaimed Sara, poking her finger at Rachel's chin. "Didn't Joel tell you?"

Rachel looked away from her. "I – I haven't seen Joel."

"You haven't?" Sara was surprised. "But he came to see you. I know he did." She smiled. "He wanted to tell you about my being his little girl!"

Rachel pushed Sara off her knee and got unsteadily to her feet. Suddenly a number of things made sense. Erica's statement that Joel had arranged the transplant, her confusion when Rachel had mentioned about James being in hospital; and most of all, James's uncertainty when he first came to see her, the uncertainty which had vanished when he realised she was unaware of the true facts. Her heart missed a beat. Was that why he had suggested they should get married at once, while she was in the hospital? It had to be. It also explained why he didn't want her to see Joel. He hadn't bargained for Sara ...

She breathed deeply. Panic, like a driving force, was rising inside her. If Sara hadn't come here – if she hadn't learned the truth, she would have married James for nothing ... for nothing ...

And yet was that entirely fair? It was not his fault that Sara had received another transplant. He had been prepared to go ahead with the arrangement. But the arrangement wasn't necessary now. Or was it?

She pressed her palms to her hot cheeks. Where did this leave her? There was still Joel; his desire to adopt Sara still hovered above her head, manifest in everything Sara had said since she came into the room. She could still marry James if she wanted to keep the child.

But could she do it? Not just because she didn't love James. If she had loved no one else, that would have been no problem? He was a likeable man in some ways, despite his ruthlessness. They might have been very happy together. But she had to think of Sara. She had to be given the chance now to choose. Joel had made her recovery possible. He had taken the decision which she, Rachel, might have hesitated about taking. She no longer had the undisputed right to the child's affections.

"Mummy?" Sara was tugging at her dressing gown. "Mummy, what's the matter?"

Rachel turned to her at once. "Nothing, darling." She drew her towards the chair again. "Sara, come and sit down. I – I have something to tell you. I must try and explain something to you."

Sara frowned. "What is it? You look cross. Are you angry with me?"

"Angry with you?" Rachel shook her head gently. "Of course not." She hugged the little girl to her. "No, I'm not angry. I just hope you won't be angry with me."

"Why should I be angry with you?" Sara frowned.

Rachel sighed. "What would you say if I told you that – that Joel was really your daddy?"

Sara gasped. "But my daddy's dead!"

"No. No, he's not. He's very much alive."

"Joel?"

Rachel nodded.

"I can't believe it." Sara's lips parted in astonishment. "He's really my daddy? But how? Why? Why aren't you living with him, then?"

Rachel shook her head. "It's a long story, Sara. But simply it means that Mummy and Daddy had a terrible argument and split up, and you lived with me, and Joel – Joel lived in London."

"But – " Sara's eyes clouded, "didn't he ever come to see me?"

Rachel bit her lip. This was going to be even more difficult than she had thought. "He – he couldn't. He didn't know anything about you."

"How?"

Rachel hesitated. "You know where babies come from, don't you, Sara? You've seen the ladies in the village when they've been expecting babies, haven't you?"

"Yes. They grow in mummies' tummies."

"Yes. Well, I didn't know you were growing in my tummy until after – after Daddy and I had split up."

Sara's face cleared. "So he knew nothing about me?"

"Not – not until just recently."

Sara beamed. "And now he knows, he wants me to be his

little girl," she said, with great satisfaction.

"Well – yes."

Sara lifted her shoulders ecstatically. "Oh, how super! And we can go and live in that lovely house that looks all over London? Do you know he has a big room there that's almost all glass where he does his painting?" she asked in an awed voice.

Rachel bent her head. "You can go and live with him if you want to, darling. Joel wants you to. But I shan't be living there with you."

"Why not?" Sara stared at her.

Rachel shook her head. "Sara, I know it's hard for you to understand, but – well, Joel and I don't – don't get on together. Besides, he has Erica – "

"Oh, *her!*" Sara made her feelings about Erica very clear in that one word. "I don't want to live with her."

"You'd be living with Joel," said Rachel steadily. "You'd be his little girl, as you said. You'd like that, wouldn't you?"

"Without you?" Sara's lips trembled. "I don't want to leave you."

Rachel sighed. "Well, there's no need for you to decide right now." She blinked back the hot tears that were burning the backs of her eyes as a thought struck her. "How did you get here anyway?"

Sara hunched her shoulders. "Dr. Lorrimer brought me." She sniffed. "He wants to see you, too."

"Does he?" Rachel put up a hand to her hair. "Then – then perhaps you'd better ask him to come in."

Sara touched her hair before sliding off her knee. "Your hair's different. Not so soft. I don't like it."

Rachel forced a faint smile. "Nor do I. It's a wig. But they had to shave off Mummy's hair to – to operate."

Sara was distracted by this idea. "You mean – you're bald?"

Rachel wished the word did not sound so stark somehow.

"You might say that," she nodded.

"Can I see?"

"Not now." Rachel pushed her towards the door. "Go and tell Mr. Lorrimer I'd like to see him now."

Sister Thomas took Sara away to have some orange juice while the surgeon spoke to Rachel about the after-effects of the operation. He explained what treatment she would need, and after ascertaining that Rachel understood him, he continued:

"Sara's been extremely lucky, you know, Mrs. Gilmour. The adult transplant would have required a lot more treatment. As it is, there's absolutely no reason why Sara shouldn't live a perfectly normal life from now on."

"I – Mr. Kingdom – Mr. *Joel* Kingdom, that is – said that suppressive drugs needed after an adult kidney transplant might have affected Sara's development."

"I'm afraid he's right. At the moment, techniques in this field are still somewhat limited. But they are improving. The transplanting of kidneys into children is still in its infancy, as it were. Potentially, it's an exciting field." He paused. "Sara has been very happy with us, I think. We've kept her in a little longer than necessary after your own accident to ensure that nothing is likely to go wrong afterwards."

"I'm very grateful to you."

"Not at all. Sara's a charming child." Mr. Lorrimer smiled, and then looked consideringly at Rachel's pale cheeks. "But I think we've stayed long enough for a first visit, don't you? You look rather strained, Mrs. Gilmour. But believe me, you have nothing to worry about."

Hadn't she? Rachel wished she could be as certain. Saying goodbye to Sara was a painful experience, and even the child seemed to sense her anxiety.

"Don't worry, Mummy," she whispered tremulously. "I won't leave you."

But lying alone in her room that night, Rachel was not so

sure. After all, if she did not marry James Kingdom, what kind of a life could she offer Sara compared with what Joel could do for her? Was love enough to compensate? Particularly as with Joel she would be loved, too?

By morning she had come to a decision. She was tired, but determined. So long as she was around to divide Sara's affections, the child would never – *could never* – be expected to make the choice in favour of Joel. It would be far simpler if she removed herself from the arena and gave Joel his chance with the child, give him back the years she had had, with interest. At some point in the future, they could meet again, and by then Sara would be old enough to know her own mind. Now her emotions ruled her head, but it would not always be so.

It was a shattering decision, and one which would require all her will power and strength of mind to carry out. But alone, she might be able to pick up the threads of her studies, and if she could bury herself in her work, time would pass. She wanted to weep when she thought of someone else looking after Sara, changing her clothes, brushing her hair, getting her ready for bed – sharing all the little intimacies which previously she had shared. But she mustn't give in to sentimentality. She deliberately hardened her resolve with cynicism. Sara would soon forget. Children were incredibly resilient. With Joel to help her, to entertain her, to take her with him wherever he went, she would soon forget about the dullness of her past in the brilliance of her future ...

CHAPTER ELEVEN

But there was still one more hurdle to face. James Kingdom.

Rachel knew she would have to see him and tell him exactly what she intended to do. It was a gruelling prospect, but he deserved to know her plans. Then, when she was able to leave the hospital, she would make arrangements to move away from London.

It was two more days before James appeared. Sara came to see her again, this time accompanied by one of the young nurses from the hospital, and it did Rachel good to see her looking so fit and well. She was obviously receiving a lot of spoiling, and was growing used to getting her own way in everything. All she wanted to do was talk about how Joel came to be her daddy, and when Rachel tried to change the subject, she became upset. By the time she left, Rachel's nerves were strung to a fine pitch.

The next morning Sister Thomas informed her that Mr. James Kingdom was here to see her. Rachel was up and dressed in the shirt, pants and waistcoat she had been wearing on the night of her accident, and when James was shown into the room he looked taken aback at the sight of her. He had strode in, confident and assured, but her appearance seemed to disconcert him.

"Why, Rachel!" he exclaimed. "I – I'm amazed. You look almost recovered!"

Rachel omitted to explain that she had spent some time over her make-up that morning, and that the colour in her cheeks owed more to artifice than natural good health.

"Well," he went on, when she said nothing, "you'll be

delighted to hear that I've made all the arrangements. We're to be married in two days from now."

"Oh, no, we're not," Rachel spoke then. "I'm afraid the situation has changed, James. You and I will not be having a wedding."

James stared at her disbelievingly. "What did you say?" His brows drew together. "What has Joel been telling you?"

"Joel's been telling me nothing. I haven't even seen Joel – as I promised." Her lips curled. "Why did you do it, James? How could you think you'd get away with it?"

James's face mirrored his consternation. "I don't know what you're talking about," he blustered.

"Oh, yes, you do, James. You didn't give Sara one of your kidneys. You were in Germany at the time she had the transplant. Some poor child who died is responsible for Sara's recovery."

James clenched his fists. "I didn't say I'd shared in the transplant, did I?"

"Equally, you didn't say that you hadn't."

"There's still Joel! He still wants to adopt Sara."

"I know that." Rachel felt suddenly very tired. "I'm going to let him do it. If he wants to."

"What?"

"It's no use, James. I've fought him long enough."

"Rachel, you don't know what you're saying – "

"I do. I've thought about it constantly for the past few days. I can't deprive him of his daughter if he really wants her."

"Rachel, this is lunacy – "

"James, ever since Sara came to see me – "

"Sara? Sara's been to see you?" James was staggered. "But how? Joel's in France! How – how could she?"

"Mr. Lorrimer brought her the first time."

"And it was she . . ."

"Yes. You should have realized. Sara is no fool. She's alert to everything going on around her."

James paced restlessly about the room. "I can't believe you mean this, Rachel. Have you thought what could happen?"

"If you mean – do I realise that Joel could alienate Sara's affections towards me, then yes, I know that. But I don't think he will. He wants the child, he wants to adopt her. But I think he realises she's sufficiently like me not to turn against her own mother!"

James shook his head. "You'll regret this."

"Probably." Rachel bent her head. "James, it hasn't been an easy decision. Don't make it any harder than it already is. All right, I know I'm letting you down, but in a sense you let me down too, when you tried to keep the truth from me. You knew – you must have guessed that that would make a difference. Oh, it's a temptation, I know. Marrying you would negate any claim Joel might have. But I can't do it. I just can't."

"He'll take her away – "

"Very probably."

"He's bought a house in France. He's going to live there. He's giving up his lucrative career here in London."

"That's nothing to do with me," she cried. But it was. It hurt. So he could give up his former life for Erica, but not for her. "I hope he'll be very happy."

James stared impotently at her. "You're determined, aren't you?"

"Yes."

"God damn him!"

James turned and strode out of the room, and only then did Rachel realise she was shaking. But it had been an exhausting interview, and she sought the safety of her chair. Well, that was it! It was over. All that was left now was to get well enough to leave hospital and pack up. She would not tell Sara she was going. That would be the best way. Farewells would tear her apart. She would leave a letter for Joel and he could explain to his daughter. *His* daughter – not *her* daughter any more.

Rachel discharged herself from the hospital three days later. She did so without the approval of Mr. Frazer, and with the genuine disapproval of Sister Thomas.

"You had a narrow escape, Mrs. Gilmour. Can't you see how foolhardy it is to risk your health now?"

Rachel had turned, putting on her jacket. "I'm grateful for your concern, Sister, but I have to go."

"And what about Sara? Do you think risking your health will help her? She's perfectly happy in the hospital until you're fully recovered."

"Sara?" Rachel pressed her lips together to prevent them from trembling. "Oh, Sara will be all right. She's going to live with her father."

Sister Thomas looked uncomfortable. "Pardon me, Mrs. Gilmour, but your husband has never been to see you."

"I don't have a husband, Sister. Just a daughter, and a lot of bitter memories." Rachel hesitated. "Joel Kingdom is Sara's father. Now do you understand?"

The flat had been cold and unwelcoming on her arrival, but she soon turned on the electric fire and opening a tin of milk made herself a cup of tea. She intended to stay at the flat overnight while she composed her letter to Joel. Tomorrow she would take what money she had out of the bank and buy a ticket for some other town.

The effort of making the tea exhausted her, however, and she had to sit down before tackling her packing. Walking round the hospital was one thing, coping with everything for herself was something else again. She would have to take a room in a hotel until she was strong enough to get a flat or a bedsitter.

In Sara's bedroom, she looked about her with sinking spirits.

Evidence of her occupation was strewn around, and Rachel bent to pick up one of the dolls, holding it close to her as tears pricked at her eyes. Then, angrily, she thrust the doll aside. She would never make anything of her life if she continually indulged herself in emotionalism.

During the afternoon she rested, and by evening she felt capable of packing a suitcase. Opening the wardrobe doors, she surveyed the array of clothes that James Kingdom had paid for. She wanted none of them. Instead she extracted her own skirts and trousers, the skirts and sweaters she had owned before coming to London. The only garments she intended keeping were those she was wearing. A foolish whim indeed to wear the clothes in which Joel had seen her for the last time.

She was in the bedroom, folding sweaters into the suitcase, when the outer door of the flat opened and she heard someone come in. For a moment her heart missed a beat and all James's stories of being alone in the flat came to haunt her. But then common sense asserted itself. Only two people had a key to the flat, apart from herself, James and Mrs. Talbot.

Taking a deep breath, she walked to the door of the bedroom just as the intruder came through the lounge to find her. But it was not James or Mrs. Talbot. It was Joel who confronted her, and Rachel fell back aghast as she realised she had taken off her wig to lie down and had not bothered to put it on again. She put up a trembling hand to her bared head, feeling the downy softness of the growth of new hair, knowing what a terrible sight she must present to the man staring so bitterly at her.

"Joel!" she breathed, finding her voice. "Wh-what do you want?"

"Oh, Rachel!" he rasped, raking a hand through his hair as he surveyed her. "Why in God's name did you discharge yourself from the hospital?" He looked past her to the open suitcase on the bed. "What the hell are you doing?"

Rachel wished she could cover her head with her hands. She was overwhelmingly conscious of the ugliness of it, and she turned, fumbling for the wig she had thrown on to the dressing table.

But Joel caught her shoulders from behind, swinging her round to face him, snatching the wig out of her hands and tossing it aside. "Answer me, Rachel! I mean to know!"

Rachel forced herself to say: "Let me put the wig on first," but he merely shook her, albeit gently.

"I don't care about the wig," he muttered savagely. "I don't care how you look. Rachel, what were you planning to do?"

She bent her head, unconsciously exposing the soft hairs on her nape to his view. "I – I was going away. Oh – " She looked up as his hands tightened, "not with Sara. I – I – I was going to write to you, but I can tell you now. Sara can stay with you – "

"What?"

"She can. She wants to. Oh, she's talked about not leaving me, but I know – "

"You know? *You know?* You don't know anything!" bit out Joel fiercely. He let her go so suddenly she almost fell, and with a muffled exclamation of pain he caught her again, pulling her into his arms, burying his face in the downy softness at the nape of her neck. He was trembling, she could feel it and because of this she didn't attempt to pull away. "Oh, Rachel!" he groaned shudderingly, "don't go away. Don't leave me! I don't think I can go on if you walk out on me again!"

Rachel dragged herself away from him then, staring at him disbelievingly. "Joel, we've been through all this – "

"No. No, we haven't." His dark eyes caressed her.

"We have." Rachel turned away, unable to look at him without wanting to go back into his arms. "Joel, I've said you can have Sara. I'm giving her to you. When – when she's old enough to decide, I'll – I'll come back."

"I won't let you do it!" he muttered, grasping her shoulders and drawing her back against him as if he couldn't bear to let her out of his arms. "Oh, Rachel, listen to me – listen to me!"

"You said you wanted to adopt Sara," she exclaimed, a little desperately, moving against him and feeling his instant response to her closeness.

"I know I did," he groaned, his mouth against her neck seducing her reason. "I do. I want to adopt Sara just as soon as we're married."

"What?" Rachel couldn't take this in. "Joel – "

"For God's sake, keep still, or I won't be able to guarantee the consequences," he breathed huskily. "Just stay there – mmm, Rachel, you've no idea how good that feels!"

Rachel could feel emotion sweeping over her body, and she exclaimed: "Joel, you said – when we were *married!*"

"I know I did." He twisted her round in his arms to look down at her. "Did you think I wouldn't? Isn't that what I've wanted all along?"

Rachel tried not to feel too disturbed. "For – for Sara's sake?" she probed.

"No," he said harshly, cupping her face in his hands. "No, not for Sara's sake! My God, Rachel, you take some convincing. Must I get down on my bended knees and ask for your hand?" He shook his head.

"W-would you do that?"

"If you wanted me to. You must know how I feel about you. I've demonstrated it so many times."

Rachel tried to take it in. "But – but – Erica – "

"I don't love Erica. I never did – I told you. I love you. I always have. When I lost you, I really suffered, believe me!"

"But I thought – your father said – "

"My father has a lot to answer for."

"But Erica – "

"I know. Erica came to see you. But I didn't know about that! How could I? I was in France. Then, when I came back, you refused to see me."

"You could have insisted."

"You don't insist when someone has been as ill as you have, Rachel." He shook his head. "I was prepared to wait. I didn't know you would do anything as crazy as discharge yourself from hospital." He shuddered. "To think – if I hadn't got back and gone to the hospital, you would have disappeared again."

"I thought that was what you wanted," she breathed, sliding her hands up his chest.

"What? After the way I showed you how I felt?"

"I – I knew you – *wanted* me. But you wanted me before, didn't you?"

"I never stopped wanting you!" he muttered, staring at her. "You've got to believe me. If you had come back – you would have known."

"But you never wanted children, Joel! You said so."

He sighed. "Yes. Well, perhaps I should tell you something, something my father should have told you. My mother died of kidney disease."

"You mean – "

"I mean, if there was any heredity involved, it was from my side of the family, not yours."

"I see."

Joel closed his eyes for a moment and then opened them again. "It's no excuse for the way I behaved, I know, but my father was a changed man after my mother died. Everyone said so. He had loved her desperately, and I made myself a promise that I'd never love anyone like that. And – and if for some reason I should find someone – I'd never get married, never have any children to destroy our relationship."

"Oh, Joel!"

"I'm not proud of myself when I think what you went through alone. I should have made sure nothing like that could happen. But with you – " He looked disturbingly at her mouth. "Well, you know what it was like. I didn't want to spoil it. But I did."

"Oh, Joel, I love you!" she breathed, and with an exclamation he covered her mouth with his own and there was no more talking for several minutes.

When at last he lifted his head, he was breathing unsteadily and his eyes were glazed as she had seen them before.

"Oh, God, Rachel, never leave me! Never leave me!" He shook his head. "This is why I wanted Sara – God forgive me! Because she's your child as well as mine. I love her – but only because she's so like you. She may look like me, but she's just like you!"

His vulnerability was very disturbing and it was with a great effort that Rachel tried to speak of more mundane things. "You – you didn't come to see me after the operation. Why not? Why did you wait until – until I had seen Erica?"

He sighed. "I went away – to France – to buy a house. A small chateau, actually. Will you share it with me – with me and my daughter?"

She stroked her fingers down his cheek. "What would you have done if I hadn't been here when you came back?"

"Gone quietly out of my mind," he stated steadily.

"You wouldn't!"

"No? I think I would. And I think my father thought I would, too."

"What do you mean?"

"He telephoned me this morning. He told me he had had a call from the hospital to the effect that you were discharging yourself today. He thought I ought to know. Obviously, the hospital couldn't let you go without informing someone."

"Oh, Joel!"

"You might well say *Oh, Joel*!" He put his mouth to the corner of hers.

"So your father turned out to be not such a villain after all?"

"I don't know about that." Joel's mouth hardened slightly. "He knew what he was doing all along. It was his way of getting back at me. If only you'd come to me in the beginning ..."

"How could I?"

Joel nodded. "I know. What was it you called me? A selfish bastard? I was – I know it. But my God, I've paid for it." He sighed. "As for my father, if I were charitable I would say that he saw Sara's illness as a means to expunge the guilt he had always felt about my mother's death. He genuinely wanted to help her – that much I do know."

"And now – "

"Well, now we get married. As soon as possible."

Rachel touched her head. "You don't mind – about this?"

Joel smiled then, a warm indulgent smile. "Why should I mind? You look like a baby."

"An overgrown baby," murmured Rachel dryly.

"Not to me." He drew her close, pressing his lips to her soft scalp. "It will grow. I like the way you look, Rachel, I don't deny it, when you're beautifully groomed and your hair is soft and silky – but it's not your looks I love. It's you, the person you are. The mother of my child – the meaning of my life."

"Sara will be delighted," she murmured, when he lifted his mouth from hers again. "To have both a mother and a father ..."

"... and a home," added Joel softly, releasing her to flex his shoulder muscles. "Now, will you move that suitcase off the bed or shall I? I'm worn out. I haven't slept for three days and nights. You have no idea of the trouble you've caused me, the night's sleep I've lost!"

"Is it worth it?" she asked, and he grinned sheepishly.

"Without a shadow of a doubt," he conceded, pulling her to him again. "Now, if I sleep here tonight, will you accuse me of taking advantage of you again . . . ?"

December Paperbacks continued

HEART IN THE SUNLIGHT
by Lilian Peake

Norway, Noelle found, when she went to work there, was a land of sunlight, glorious scenery and charming people—with the exception, unfortunately, of her boss, the infuriating Per Arneson!

SOUTH OF CAPRICORN
by Anne Hampson

Gail had been deeply fond of her cousin Sandra, and when Sandra died, leaving a small daughter who had been disowned by her father, she vowed to take the child out to Australia and seek him out. But when she actually met Kane Farrell she realised that it was not going to be quite as simple as that . . .

ROSS OF SILVER RIDGE
by Gwen Westwood

Ross Trent wanted a nice cosy middle-aged woman to take charge of the three young children in his care—but instead he got Taryn Bartlett, who was twenty but looked five years younger. Ross was not pleased, his glamorous girlfriend Coral was even less pleased. How long would Taryn last?

DEEP FURROWS
by Sue Peters

Lorne loved her job of restoring a beautiful old country house. But as time went by she also realised that she loved the owner, Guy Noble—who was preparing to marry a most unsuitable girl. But that was just Lorne's opinion, wasn't it? There was certainly no future for her as far as Guy was concerned . . .

THE SWEET SURRENDER
by Rose Burghley

David Falcon was plagued by adoring women. But one girl disliked him strongly, so he picked her as a watchdog to keep off the others. It was a move that was destined to defeat itself.

30p net each

Available December 1975